"Please let me go, Chay."

Sophie whispered the plea, her eyes huge.

"Don't do that!" Chay lifted his hand to her heated cheek, to graze it with his thumb. "Or I'll have to kiss you again...until you beg me to let you stay."

"You've got a great notion of your physical attraction," she declared roundly.

"Have I? Are you confident enough of your willpower to put it to the test?"

Liz Fielding was born in Berkshire, England, and educated at a convent school in Maidenhead. At twenty she took off for Africa to work as a secretary in Lusaka, where she met her civil engineer husband, John. They spent the following ten years working in Africa and the Middle East. She began writing during the long evenings when her husband was working away on contract. Liz and her husband are now settled in Wales with their children, Amy and William.

Prisoner of
the Heart
Liz Fielding

Harlequin Books

TORONTO • NEW YORK • LONDON
AMSTERDAM • PARIS • SYDNEY • HAMBURG
STOCKHOLM • ATHENS • TOKYO • MILAN
MADRID • WARSAW • BUDAPEST • AUCKLAND

ISBN 0-373-17277-X

PRISONER OF THE HEART

First North American Publication 1996.

Copyright © 1995 by Liz Fielding.

Printed in U.S.A.

CHAPTER ONE

'GOT you, Chay Buchanan!' Sophie Nash's triumphant exclamation was a tightly contained whisper. Perched on a rocky ledge fifty feet above a rock-strewn bay, she had waited too long—all an apparently endless afternoon, while the sun had crept around the headland, stealing her shade, beating into the exposed crevice with barely enough room to ease her aching back or flex her legs—to risk giving herself away now.

And she had almost given up. The sun was sinking fast, taking with it the precious light. Another ten minutes, she had promised herself, and she would end the torture and climb the fifteen or so feet back up to the top of the cliff. She had pressed herself a little closer to the comfort of the rock-face. The ledge had seemed larger viewed from the safety of the cliff-top and she had been so certain that she would be able to see the wide expanse of terrace between the tower and the sea. But she had been wrong. Only the tantalising glimpse of the pool had kept her riveted to her eyrie, praying that the sudden rise in temperature would tempt her quarry out for a swim. And finally it had.

The man fixed in her sights was staring out to sea, his hand raised against the westering sun. She released the shutter and the motor-wind drove the film forward as the wind whipped up a dark lock of hair and feathered it across his forehead. He was relaxed now, at ease in the safety of his keep. All that would change if he discovered that he was being observed. She shivered involuntarily, despite the heat. He had made himself more than clear. Warned her to stay away. Warned her that if she was ever unfortunate enough to be found anywhere near the old watch-tower that was his home with a camera in her possession she would discover that the dungeon was still a working feature.

Sophie shrugged away the disquieting thought of being locked inside the dark recesses of his tower. He had been simply melodramatic, trying to scare her off. Well, he would find out that she didn't scare off that easily. His dungeon was undoubtedly nothing more threatening than a wine cellar these days. Besides, she wasn't trespassing. There wasn't a thing he could do to her. Oh, no? The thought was in her head before she could stop it. No! His property began on the other side of the great overhanging rock that so effectively protected his privacy. All but the pool at the sea's edge. And he would never know she had been there until the photographs appeared alongside Nigel's feature in *Celebrity*.

She twisted the zoom lens, closing in on the tanned profile and a pair of well-made shoulders, naked but for the towel thrown about them. The skin of his back gleamed like bronze silk in the early evening sun, smooth, packed with muscle, like an ancient statue of an athlete she had seen once in a museum. Her mouth dried as she panned the lense downwards, but the briefest black swimsuit clung to his hips, and the smallest gasp of something that might have been relief escaped her lips.

She quickly swung the long lens back up to his face, almost jumping as she adjusted the focus and he suddenly appeared close enough to touch. That first sense of triumph evaporated as she acknowledged that her response to such compelling masculinity, even at this distance, was as immediate and disturbing as on their first encounter. She felt a hot, remembering flush of shame at the way his knowing eyes had declined the imagined invitation.

He wasn't even handsome, Sophie thought furiously. Chay Buchanan possessed no feature that might lay claim to such an adjective. His face was rugged, lived-in. No, slept-in. She shifted, uncomfortable with the memory of the naïve way she had knocked at the door of his fortress to ask if he would let her take a photograph of him. She should have known that it couldn't possibly be that simple or Nigel would never have asked her. . . Her foot disturbed a small shower of stones and in a sudden panic, sure that the whole world must hear, she flattened herself against the cliff and held her breath as they rattled down to the sea.

But there was no shout of rage and finally she braved a peek over the ledge. He hadn't moved, his fierce profile fixed upon a distant yacht, sails straining against the wind as it cut through the brilliant blue of the Mediterranean.

Turn, she willed the man. Look this way. If he would just turn towards her, every painful, cramping moment on the ledge would be worthwhile. And turn he did, as if her mind had somehow reached out and touched his.

She took a deep, steadying breath as the lens was filled with that unforgettable face. Dark brows jutted fiercely over the sea-green eyes that this morning had seemed to bore into her to search out her secrets, and she had to remind herself very firmly that he had no idea that she had found a chink in his armour and was at this very moment intruding on his seclusion. If he had, he certainly wouldn't be standing relaxed and at ease at the edge of his pool.

Chay Buchanan had made it only too plain that trespassers were not welcome, and she wondered briefly if his nose had been broken defending that privacy. The most recent library photographs of the man had been more than six years old. He had been standing grim-faced at his brother's graveside, and in that shot his nose had been arrow-straight.

It had been set without much thought as to the aesthetics of the matter, and with his sun-darkened skin it gave him the hawkish look of a corsair. Just the kind of man to keep his enemies in a dungeon, Sophie thought uncomfortably. His mouth was wide and might be pleasing when he smiled. She wouldn't know. When she had seen it last it had been little more than a thin angry slash over an uncompromising chin. She released the shutter and claimed the image for her own.

He pulled the towel from around his neck, and dropped it on the rocks at his feet. Her finger hovered over the shutter release, capturing the moment of sheer power and grace as his body unwound and he dived into the water of a pool carved out of the rocks, fed and cleaned by a narrow channel from the sea.

With a series of workmanlike pictures of the reclusive writer safely on film, Sophie leaned back against the rock to catch her breath. A slight frown creased her brow as she watched the man carving his way through the water.

Chay Buchanan had once strutted the literary stage like a young lion, the darling of the media. But it was years since he had appeared on every prestigious arts programme as the literary find of the century. Years since his last book had done the almost impossible feat of flying to the top of the bestseller lists in London and New York before capturing one of the greatest literary prizes on offer.

Since then, nothing. No more books to win prestigious prizes and fly to the top of the bestseller lists. No more photographs of him accompanied by beautiful women to fill the gossip pages. He had simply disappeared.

According to Nigel, he had turned his back on the world, sold his London home and retreated to this island fastness. With an up-to-date photograph it would make a good feature. Long on speculation, short on facts. He was an ideal target for the kind of magazine that lived off scandal and well-known faces.

Sophie's fingers tightened around the cassette of film as she anticipated what would be done with her photographs. After this morning she had no reason to feel anything but antipathy for the man yet, slightly sickened by what she had done, she had to resist a sudden urge to fling the thing into the sea. She hated magazines like *Celebrity*. Sophie eased her shoulders, pushed back a wayward strand of fair hair that had escaped her plait to cling clammily to her forehead and watched her quarry, now slicing relentlessly through the water.

She stared down at the cassette, then, before she could do anything so utterly stupid, she dropped it into the button-down pocket of her shirt. She had no choice, she reminded herself. If Chay Buchanan had nothing to hide then Nigel couldn't hurt him. And she very firmly shut out the insistent voice that told her she was fooling herself.

Automatically she reloaded the camera with film, her eyes straying once more to the powerful figure of Chay Buchanan. But he had stopped the apparently effortless crawl and was lying on his back in the water, looking back towards the tower. Sophie watched, almost mesmerised by the beauty of his body glistening through the sheen of water as it rose and fell against the restless sea surging through the narrow gap in the rock. A tiny crease furrowed her forehead as she frowned, wondering what he was doing. Then, with a jolt, she knew, almost froze, as a buzz of excitement rippled her skin to gooseflesh. He was watching someone. There was someone else on the terrace.

She flattened herself as close to the edge of her rocky perch as she dared and strained to see. Who was it? A woman? Please, please, she begged the kindly Fates, let it be a woman. Someone famous. A well-known actress. A model. Something sensational enough to make up for not getting inside the tower, something that would please Nigel enough to hand over that precious envelope. . . And if it was somebody else's wife? Her conscience jabbed at her. She pushed the thought to one side. This was not the moment to dwell on moral dilemmas. She would worry about that later. Right now, if she didn't keep her head, there would be no photographs.

She hung over the edge a little, blotting out the dizzying drop to the sea in her effort to gain a few extra inches of terrace, but the great overhang of rock that protected the tower from prying eyes was still obstructing her view. Chay Buchanan raised his arms in encouragement to his unseen companion and a flash of white teeth confirmed that he was laughing. And she had been right about his mouth. Long seconds passed before she remembered her task and captured the moment on film.

A sudden movement galvanised her into action, but the body that leapt into those inviting arms was no famous beauty. It was a child. A dark-haired, straight-limbed boy, five or maybe six years old, and as at home in the water as his father. For a moment surprise held her transfixed. There could be no mistake in the relationship, the likeness was too marked. But Nigel had said nothing about a child. Or a wife. And Chay Buchanan certainly hadn't had the look of a married man.

She shook away the thought and the film ripped through the spool as she kept her finger on the release. With almost trembling fingers she dropped the used film into her bag and fed in another. There was barely enough light now for long-range photography. The sun was dipping relentlessly towards the sea, but still she carried on, her eye glued to the camera and the two figures framed in the viewfinder. Then she saw the boy pointing towards the cliff. Towards her.

Chay Buchanan's eyes creased as he scoured the cliff, and the mouth once again became that angry slash as the lowering sun gleamed against the hooded lens, betraying her. For a particle of a second their eyes clashed as the distance that separated them shrank to nothing.

There was no hurry, she told her trembling fingers as she flipped the film from the camera. By the time he was dry and dressed and halfway to the cliff-top, where her car was hidden from casual view, she would be gone. There was plenty of time. She repeated the words over and over in her head like a mantra. Just a short, easy climb and she was away. But her hands trembled a little as she hurriedly pushed her camera into the soft cocoon in her carrying bag. She slung it over her shoulder, glanced up at the route she had to take and reached for the first handhold.

It was unexpectedly difficult. Hours of being cramped, unable to stretch properly, had left her stupidly weak, and her legs began to tremble as she forced them to push her upwards, and her hands slipped sweatily on the suddenly elusive handholds as she thought of Chay Buchanan hurrying to intercept her. She was forced to stop, draw deep breaths into her lungs, remind herself that it was easy. She hadn't been about to kill herself over a few photographs. If it had been dangerous she would never have risked it.

Not even for Jennie? The thought of her sister lent her fresh strength. She had seen the way clearly down to the ledge. Now it was simply a matter of keeping her head, forgetting the drop below her and climbing back up to the cliff path before Chay Buchanan got there. The thought of meeting him again urged her on.

She clenched her teeth as the pain burned in her forearms. And with every agonising inch up the cliff-face she cursed Chay Buchanan. All she wanted was one photograph, a simple portrait to illustrate Nigel's article. And she had asked politely. If he hadn't been so damned rude she might have taken his refusal. It wasn't her way to sneak around corners, taking pictures of people who would rather be left alone. But a stab of guilt seared her cheeks as she recalled the extraordinary thrill of triumph when she had had the man in her sights.

Her fingertips reached upwards; she was desperate now for the ledge. Surely she was nearly there? But fifteen feet suddenly seemed more like fifty as there was just more rock to tear at her nails and scrape the skin from her fingers. Going down, it had all seemed so simple. Plenty of footholds. No more daunting than the bank in the local park where she and Jennie had played as children. The difference being that when she had slipped in the park there hadn't been a vertiginous drop down a sea-lashed cliff. Stop it! she warned her imagination. If she fell she would crash back on to the ledge. Nasty, painful—that was all. *All*? And if she hit her head? Rolled off?

Panic made her glance up, and her shift in weight almost undid her. She threw herself back at the rock-face, closing her eyes to shut out the dizzy spinning, and for the first time felt real fear cold-feather her spine. She clung on, wondering just how long she could stay there before the pain in her arms and the trembling weakness in her legs became too much and she simply fell.

'Can I offer you a hand, Sophie Nash?'

Her whole body lurched with shock at the harsh invitation. Taking great care not to overbalance, she glanced up once more, to find herself being regarded by a pair of fathomless eyes. He had flattened himself against the ground and stretched a hand down towards her. So close? She had been that close? She felt like weeping with frustration. But pride kept the tears at bay. Instead she glared at the strong, square hand and quite deliberately ignored the proferred lifeline. 'I can manage,' she ground out, and, as if to demonstrate this, grabbed the nearest rocky protrusion to ease herself up another few inches.

'I really think you should take my hand,' he advised coldly. 'I won't drop you, despite the undoubted provocation.'

But this small triumph had given her new heart. Adrenalin surging through her veins, she made another foot of height before she was forced once more to stop. She pressed her cheek against the rapidly cooling rock and tried to ease the strain on her limbs and drag air into her lungs through her parched throat. She hadn't known it was possible to hurt so much.

'Don't be stubborn, Sophie.' His voice was urgent now. 'You're not going to make it without help.'

His hawkish face was nearer, the lines carved deep into his cheeks, and he reached for her. 'Leave me alone,' she gasped, but the words were little more than a croak.

'Fine words. Remember them,' he ordered, 'if you live long enough.'

'I can manage!' she repeated, the words turning into a scream when her foot slipped and her forehead collided sharply against the rock as she scrabbled with her toe for a hold to halt the sickening slip. She was jerked to an agonised halt as Chay Buchanan's hands grasped her wrist and he hauled her over the edge, grabbing her in a vice-like grip as he rolled away from the yawning chasm.

'You've dislocated my arm!' she complained bitterly, as the pain of torn muscles brought tears swimming to her eyes.

'You would rather have fallen?' She didn't answer, couldn't answer through pain and tears. 'And I haven't dislocated anything.' He moved her arm, none too gently, and she groaned involuntarily and let her head fall forward on to his naked chest. 'See? Still in working order. No thanks to you.'

No wonder he had been so quick to reach her, she thought. He hadn't bothered to dry himself or put on more than a pair of shorts. But she was too weak with pain and exhaustion to move. Instead she lay very still, her cheek pressed against the dark hair that stippled his chest, listening to the steady thud of his heartbeat, while she tried to recover her strength. But he wasn't finished with her yet.

'You have dangerous hobbies, Sophie Nash.' He grasped her plait and yanked up her head, forcing her to confront him. 'But then, it isn't a hobby, is it?' She yelped and fresh tears started to her eyes, but he didn't care. His grasp only tightened, so that it was impossible to move without pain. 'Nevertheless, climbing alone, without a safety line, is just about the most stupid, reckless. . .' He stopped, clearly too angry to continue. Really angry. Those pirate's eyes were fierce enough to kill. 'Does anyone know where you are? If you'd fallen would anyone ever have known what had happened to you?'

How could he be so utterly heartless? Surely he must see that she was in agony? 'Someone would have found my car,' she gasped out.

'Someone would have found your car?' he repeated, in utter disbelief. '"Here lie some bits and pieces of

Sophie Nash. We know it was her because we found her car." Some epitaph.' Then the fact that silent tears were by now pouring down her face and on to his chest apparently penetrated, because he loosened his grasp of her hair and she almost whimpered with relief. But he hadn't finished. 'Let me tell you, girl, that you don't have much of a career as a paparazzo ahead of you if you ignore the simplest safety precautions.'

'I'm not a paparazzo,' she protested.

'You're giving a very good impression of one. For God's sake, is a photograph of me so valuable that it's worth risking your life? Whoever commissioned you must have promised to pay you a very great deal of money.' He frowned, then rolled over, pinning her against the rock-hard ground, crushing her breasts against his naked chest until she could hardly breathe. 'Who was it, Sophie?'

Pay? He thought she would do this for *money*? Days trailing around holiday resorts at the crack of dawn when they were deserted, making the best of hotels so that they should look exotic and desirable holiday destinations, that was what she was paid for.

Her attempt to get a photograph of the great Chay Buchanan while she was on the island had not been for the vast sums paid to professional paparazzi. It had been for something infinitely more precious. For a moment she was tempted to tell him. Ask him. . . She met his eyes and hope died. Chay Buchanan hadn't just turned her down when she had wanted to take his photograph. He had been. . .contemptuous. Anger, determination, sheer bloody-mindedness, had blinded her to the folly, the very real risk, of what she was doing.

She lay, too weak to move, her head thudding with pain from his maltreatment of her scalp. More likely the bang on your forehead, that know-it-all inner voice immediately contradicted her. She would have liked to touch the tender spot, check it out to assess the damage, but his weight fixed her to the spot and she lay quite helpless. She opened her lids to meet the angry onslaught of his eyes.

'Well?' he demanded.

She had been stupid. She knew it, was prepared to admit it. To herself. But she certainly wasn't going to give him the satisfaction of telling him so. And she wasn't going to tell him about Nigel. She had the feeling that Nigel wouldn't like that at all.

'I wanted a photograph of you to hang on my bedroom wall,' she managed to snap out. 'I'm a fan.'

For a moment he seemed taken aback. Then his lips curved in a parody of a smile. 'I don't think so, Miss Nash. I believe it would take a great deal more than that to send you down that cliff.'

'You're too modest, Mr Buchanan. Besides, it was easy enough,' she gasped, but the pain in her shoulder, her head, and torn and bleeding hands made a liar of her. Easy enough getting down.

'Easy?' he sneered. 'If it had been easy you wouldn't be lying here, you would be racing to Luqa airport now with your ill-gotten gains.'

She lay back against the hard rock. He was right, of course, and now he would take the films and she would have to tell Nigel she had failed, appeal to his sense of honour. A hollow little voice suggested that Nigel was not overburdened with the stuff. But Chay Buchanan mustn't know how much it mattered.

'I wasn't in a hurry,' she said, as if strolling up a rockface was an everyday occurrence. 'I was. . .admiring the view,' she added, with a slightly wobbly attempt at airiness.

'You won't admit it, will you?' he replied, clearly infuriated by this unrepentant display of bravado. Then he eased himself away from her, letting his eyes trail insolently from a pair of clear grey eyes, by way of a very ordinary nose and a full, over-large mouth, to linger on a bosom that rose and fell far too rapidly. 'But you're right about one thing. There's absolutely nothing wrong with the view.'

Sophie felt the colour flood to her face as she realised just how vulnerable she was. Pinned to the ground by his body, she had made not the slightest effort to free herself. 'How. . .how dare you?' she blustered, attempting to fling herself away from him, but he had her effortlessly pinioned between a pair of powerful thighs.

'Don't go all shy on me, Sophie. This morning you were quite prepared to offer me anything I wanted for that photograph.'

'That's not true! Let me go!' she demanded. Then, breathlessly, as his fingers brushed against her breast and the tip involuntarily tightened to his touch, she squeaked, 'What are you doing?' her grey eyes widening in alarm. 'Stop it!'

'You don't really mean that, Sophie Nash,' he said, knowing eyes dwelling momentarily on the tell-tale peaks thrusting against the thin white cotton of her shirt. 'There's no need to be embarrassed. Sex is the obvious response to a brush with death. It's simply nature's prompting to ensure the perpetuation of the species. But I'm afraid that right now I have something else on my mind.'

He flipped open the button of her breast-pocket and removed the film she had stowed there for safety. Then, without haste, not deliberately touching her but making no effort to avoid the inevitable intimacy, he thoroughly searched the rest of her pockets, while she squirmed with embarrassment. 'Just one roll?' he said at last.

She swallowed, then, very slowly, she nodded. For a moment he stared at her and she held her breath, certain that he would challenge her, would see the blatant lie. But her cheeks were already flaming from the intimacy of his touch and apparently satisfied he stood up, pulling her to her feet and half supporting her as her legs refused to work properly. He propelled her back towards the edge of the cliff.

'No!' She tried to step back but he held her fast, and she was too frightened of falling to attempt to jerk free. 'What. . .are you going to do?' He didn't answer, but took one gashed and bleeding hand, placed the spool of film into it and wrapped her stiff, rapidly swelling fingers around it. She glanced up at him uncertainly.

'Throw it into the sea, Sophie Nash,' he commanded, his words eerily echoing her own thoughts as she had perched on the ledge. But that had been before his hands had ransacked her pockets without a thought for her feelings. And his feelings? her over-active conscience prompted. But she was in no mood to listen to such stuff. He had no feelings. He was just a great big bully.

'No!' She defied him.

His hand gripped her arm more tightly. 'Do as I say.'

'No, damn you. I worked hard for those pictures. Do your own dirty work.'

'That's rich, coming from someone who spies on other people for a living. Throw it!' For a long moment she outfaced him, chin high, eyes blazing. 'Throw it!' he demanded.

Slowly, almost against her will, she turned to stare down at the white sea boiling around the rocks. It was oddly hypnotic, almost mesmerising. She began to sway towards it, only to be snapped back by Chay with a fierce oath. With a faint moan she turned and buried her face in his chest, and for a moment he held her and she knew he had been right. She could so easily have fallen.

And he was right about something else. Held against the warmth of his chest, almost drowning in the scent of his skin, the sharp tang of sweat and sea-water so strong that she could almost taste the salt, she wanted him to pull her down to the ground and take her, right there in the open air, with the sound of the sea pounding in her ears. The knowledge was as brutal as a slap in the face.

Horrified by desire so raw she could practically taste it, she tore herself away from him on legs weak from more than the terror of falling. It was far more frightening than that. She had to get away from this man. As quickly as possible, and not just because of her appalling reaction to him. He had found one film but she might still get away with the others. Might still snatch her moment of triumph.

She bent to pick up her bag, wincing as its weight bit into her fingers, staggering a little as the ground dipped and swayed. The feeling was beginning to come back to her hands with a vengeance, the cuts and grazes stinging viciously and making her feel nauseous.

'Nice try, Sophie. But I'll have the film.' He caught her wrist, turning her roughly, and for a moment she thought he had guessed. But he forced open her fingers, still curled tightly around the little cassette, and she cried out involuntarily. For a moment he stared at her hand, then with a sharp impatient movement he said, 'You'd better come inside and clean these.'

'I'm all right,' she protested hoarsely. He hadn't suspected. 'I'll go back to my hotel,' she said quickly. Except that she'd already checked out. Her bags were in the car. She would be driving straight to the airport where she could clean up and change back into the pristine two-piece she had been wearing when she had called on him earlier. And, once she was inside the departure lounge, she would be beyond his reach.

'You think you can drive in that state?' he uttered in disbelief.

'It's nothing,' she said desperately. All she wanted was to get to the car and sit down for a moment, until this sickening weakness passed. She paused. 'I suppose I should thank you for saving me,' she added, a little grudgingly.

'Yes, you should,' he ground out. 'But we're so far beyond the niceties of good manners that I'd prefer it if you didn't bother.'

Hackles rose at his sharp, contemptuous tone. 'I won't! In fact, Mr Buchanan, you can rest assured that I won't bother you ever again.'

'I wish I could believe that, Sophie Nash. Why don't I?' His eyes fastened on the bag biting painfully into her shoulder, and before she could prevent him he had slipped it away from her and was hefting it thoughtfully. 'Perhaps I'd better keep this to be on the safe side.'

Her grey eyes widened in horror and she flung herself at him, making a grab for the bag. 'No!' she cried as he effortlessly whisked it out of her reach. Everything spun horribly from the sudden movement.

'No?' he enquired.

'It's just my camera. I can't work without it.'

'That is supposed to appeal to my better nature? Frankly, I can't think of anything that would please me more.'

'I doubt you have a better nature!' she flung at him.

'Then you are beginning to show some sense at last.' He glanced at the bag. 'This is just your camera? You went to a lot of trouble for just one roll of film. How long were you down on the ledge?'

'Hours,' she admitted. 'But you were only there for a few minutes.'

'True. But how long does it take with a motor-drive?'

'Not long,' she admitted. Then she took a gamble. 'In fact there are about sixty exposed films in my bag. I've been working all week for a tour company, taking pictures for next year's brochures.'

'You expect me to believe that?' he asked.

Her hands were beginning to throb horribly and she lifted them in a helpless little gesture. 'Why not? It's the truth.' She swallowed as saliva began to flood her mouth. Another moment and she knew she would be sick. If only he would let her go so that she could just sit down for a minute. But he was relentless.

'Come on, Sophie Nash. You can't expect me to believe that you would risk all that work?' he said incredulously.

'Risk?' Nothing was making much sense. She was the one who had been at risk.

'You might have dropped your bag while you were climbing down.'

'I. . .' She blinked as he began to recede. 'I was very careful.' She took a step, but the ground seemed to be made of foam rubber. Surprised, she reached out a hand to steady herself and he caught it.

'What is it?'

'I'm sorry.' Her voice seemed to come from a long way off. 'I'm afraid I'm going to be. . .' She lifted her hand to her head and saw the blood running down her fingers. Then, mercifully, everything went black.

CHAPTER TWO

SOPHIE woke with a throbbing head and dry mouth, every part of her aching. The room was dim, what light there was slanting through two pairs of louvred shutters closed on tall windows. She raised her wrist to see what time it was and heard a groan. It was a moment or two before she realised the sound had come from her own lips.

She stared at bruised, swollen fingers, that looked as if they might have been through a wringer, and winced. Her fingers. And memory began to rush back, a little confused, but with the basic facts intact. The slow motion nightmare as she had tried to make it to the cliff-top. And she had nearly made it. Would have made it. Only Chay Buchanan had been waiting for her.

She looked around her at the strange room and then with a rush of horror she knew. She was in the lion's den. Worse. She groaned, and this time the response was quite deliberate. She was in the lion's bed.

The thought was enough to drag her protesting body from the smooth linen sheet, but as she propped herself against the great carved bedhead and the sheet slipped from her body something else became startlingly obvious. She was naked. She gingerly grasped the sheet between her fingers and lifted it. Utterly naked. Someone had undressed her.

Who? It seemed vitally important that she remember. Then, rather hurriedly, she blotted out the thought before she did. She didn't want to contemplate the possibility of her unconscious body being undressed by

22

Chay Buchanan. Instead she focused her attention on her surroundings.

She was in a long, wide room, the stone walls painted matt white, with two large panels, glowing blue-green abstractions of the sea, the only decoration. The floor was of some dark polished wood. On it were laid rich Bukhara rugs, barred with faint stripes of light that filtered through louvred shutters closed over floor-to-ceiling windows. Apart from the bed, flanked by night-tables and a pair of tall Chinese lamps, the only furniture was an enormous chest of drawers with heavy brass handles and an equally impressive wardrobe. A man's room. Completely devoid of any woman's touch.

She rose unsteadily, dragged the sheet from the bed, clumsily wrapped it about her with fingers that refused to bend properly and staggered to the bathroom at the far end of the room. Halfway there she questioned her knowledge that it was a bathroom, but with the question came the all too shocking answer. She remembered. And blushed hot and painfully at the memory.

He had brought her here. She had been dimly aware of being carried up a wide staircase. Then he had propped her up and the sudden rush of water had brought her gasping back to life as he had stood with her in the enormous shower-stall, stripping her while the cascade of warm water had washed away dust and sweat and blood.

She tried to swallow, but her tongue seemed to cleave to the roof of her mouth as she remembered how, too weak to stand unaided, she had simply leaned against him, her head against his shoulder, her breasts startlingly white against the dark tan of his chest. She had been incapable of protest as he had held her around the waist and briskly soaped her with a huge sponge, rinsed her, dried her and wrapped her in a soft white bathrobe and bathed her hands with antiseptic, his fingers gentle, even if the straight, hard lines of his mouth and his angry eyes had made his feelings more than plain.

The mirror alongside the bath reflected bright spots of colour that rouged her cheeks like patches on a rag doll's face against the whiteness of her skin, the pale gold shock of hair. And he had threatened her with a dungeon. She had the unnerving feeling that his dungeon would be far safer than his bathroom.

But one question was answered. There was no Mrs Buchanan. No wife, however tolerant, would have put up with such goings on. She glanced around, and the lack of feminine accoutrements confirmed the fact that whoever usually shared Chay Buchanan's king-sized bed she certainly wasn't a permanent fixture. She forced herself to her feet and opened the bathroom cabinet. Not even constant enough to have left a toothbrush. She quickly closed the door. It was none of her business, she told herself firmly.

But it was too late to blot out the image of his personal toiletries, his exquisite taste in cologne, the fact that he used an open razor.

'Have you seen enough? Or do you want the guided tour?'

She spun round, then wished she hadn't as the room lurched sickeningly. She leaned momentarily against the cool richness of Catalan tiles that decorated the wall. Then, as she followed the direction of his eyes, tugged desperately at the sheet, which had shifted alarmingly as she turned, a sudden coolness warned her that it had left her rear exposed. She edged sideways as she caught her reflection in the mirror alongside the bath. How on earth had she got that bruise on her shoulder? She lifted it slightly and the pain brought instant recall of the tearing jerk as he had hauled her over the edge of the cliff to safety.

'I was looking for some painkillers,' she said, with a brave attempt at dignified suffering.

His lip curled derisively. 'Of course you were.' He took her arm and led her firmly back to the bed. 'Lie down and I'll bring you something.'

'I'm not an invalid.'

'No, just a pain in the backside. But you'd better lie down before you fall down.' She sat down abruptly on the bed, but only because her legs were so wobbly. It was nothing to do with his telling her to and she stubbornly refused the cool enticement of a down pillow.

'If you'll bring my clothes, I'll stop being a pain in the——' she started angrily, then stopped, gathered herself a little. She couldn't afford to aggravate the man any further. 'If you'll bring my clothes, I'll be happy to leave,' she said, with exaggerated politeness.

'Please?' he suggested.

For a moment her large grey eyes snapped dangerously. 'Do I have to beg for my own clothes?' she demanded. He didn't reply, merely waited. And waited. Apparently she did. 'Please,' she ground out through clenched teeth.

'That's better. But I'm afraid your clothes are being washed. Perhaps you can have them tomorrow.'

'Tomorrow! But I have a plane to catch——'

'*Had* a plane to catch. I contacted the airport and cancelled your booking.'

'You did what?' she exclaimed, ignoring the sharp reminder that scythed through her head that anything much above a whisper was inadvisable. 'You had no right to do that!' No right to go through her handbag. Look at her personal things.

'Since you were in no position to use it, and since it's an open ticket, I thought you might be grateful to have the opportunity to re-book. I suppose I should have known better.'

'I'm fine!' she declared, with a careless disregard for the truth. 'You can keep your washing. I'm leaving.' She rose a little shakily, hitching the sheet up and taking a step in the direction of the door only to find him barring her way. 'Right now,' she said.

He immediately stood back and offered her the door. 'As you please. I moved your car into the garage.'

Along with her suitcase with all her clothes. She would have liked to march out, chin high, but the wretched sheet made that impossible. She was all too aware of a mocking little smile twisting his mouth as she edged sideways and backed towards the door. He made no move to stop her but watched her attempt at a dignified departure with scarcely veiled amusement, and suddenly she knew it couldn't be that easy. She halted uncertainly.

'But?' she demanded.

'But,' he agreed, his green pirate eyes glinting wickedly. 'Alas, the keys are not with it. But maybe you're a dab hand with a hot wire? In your job I imagine it would come in useful.'

'Of course not!'

'No? What a pity. Perhaps you should learn. Then again, you would still have the problem of clothes. Because I removed your bag, too. For safe-keeping. Or maybe you don't mind arriving at a hotel wearing nothing but that rather ineffectual attempt at a sarong.'

She clutched the sheet a little tighter, unwilling to risk dropping it from stiff fingers if she tried to wrap it around her more thoroughly.

'And since time seems to have passed rather more rapidly than you imagine, I have to inform you that the plane you are so eager to catch left several hours ago.'

Sophie stared at him, then turned to the windows

and the light filtering through the shutters. 'How long have I been here?' she demanded. 'What time is it?' She dropped a glance to her wrist. 'Is my watch in the laundry too?' Not waiting for his answer, no longer caring about modesty—after all, he'd already seen a great deal more than her backside—she swept across the room and threw open one of the shutters to admit a whisper of light and stared out. The sea was flat calm, a pale milky blue under a thin veil of mist that curtained the sun. An early-morning sun.

'I've been here all night?' But it wasn't really a question. The slightly unnerving answer was confronting her.

'All night, Sophie Nash,' he affirmed. 'Wouldn't that have made an exciting caption for your photographs? "My night with Chay Buchanan,"' he offered, with just enough conviction to bring the colour flooding to her pale complexion.

'Don't be ridiculous. I didn't spend the night with you,' she said, but her mouth was dry and she steadfastly refused to give in to the temptation to turn and check the other pillow for evidence that the bed had been occupied by two.

'You did, but it's all a matter of intepretation, isn't it? And the doctor insisted that someone must keep an eye on you.'

Her eyes flew wide open and this time she could not help herself. But the swift involuntary glance at the huge bed told her nothing. 'An eye on me?' she asked huskily.

'In case of concussion.' His long fingers combed back the tangle of sun-bleached curls from her forehead and he lightly touched the dark shadow of a bruise. 'You took quite a knock, Sophie Nash.'

She winced, raised her own hand to the spot and felt the slight swelling. She drew a long shuddering breath,

whether from the pain or the cool touch of his fingers
she could not have told—perhaps didn't want to know.
But she did know that it wasn't possible for her to stay
a moment longer in Chay Buchanan's tower. She drew
herself up to her full height, and five feet and six inches
in her bare feet had never felt quite so insubstantial.
'Then I really mustn't put you to any more trouble, Mr
Buchanan,' she said with all the dignitiy she could
muster, wrapped inadequately as she was in nothing
but a sheet. 'I should like to go now.'

'That isn't possible. Even if I were prepared to let
you go, you're in no fit state to travel. But if you do as
you're told and get back into bed I'll go and fetch some
of the painkillers the doctor left.'

Doctor? It was the second time he had mentioned a
doctor, but she didn't remember one. She must have
taken a much harder crack on the head than she had
thought. But right now that didn't matter. There was
something far more important to get straight. 'What do
you mean?' She dug her toes into the rug as he took
her arm, resisting his firm urging towards the bed. 'If
you were prepared to let me go. . .? You can't keep
me here against my will. That's. . .' Her mouth dried.
'That's kidnapping.'

'Is it?' Heavy lids drooped slightly, concealing the
expression in his eyes. 'Would you like me to ask the
local constabulary to despatch an officer to listen to
your complaint?' he offered, with every evidence of
civility. But there was a muscle working dangerously at
the corner of his mouth.

'Yes!' she flung defiantly, daring him to do just that.

He nodded. 'If you'll excuse me.' He gestured
vaguely and walked to the door.

'But. . .' She took an uncertain step after him.
'You're really going to do it?'

'Of course. Kidnapping is a very serious charge,' he

said crisply. 'You should press it home with all the force at your command.'

'I will,' she declared. Then her challenge faltered under his unwavering gaze. 'Why do I feel another "but" coming on?'

'Could it be that common sense has suggested that you were about to make a fool of yourself?'

'Why should it do that?' she demanded.

'Just think about it for a moment,' he instructed her. 'Think about the fact that I rescued you from a very dangerous situation. That I——'

'I could have managed!'

He didn't even bother to comment on the absurdity of that remark, but continued as if she hadn't spoken. 'That I brought you to my home, bathed your wounds——'

'And a great deal else.' She flushed as his mouth curved in a provoking little smile. Stupid. Stupid to have mentioned that. Why couldn't she have forgotten that?

'I bathed your wounds,' he repeated, 'before I put you into my own bed and sent for a doctor, who advised several days of rest.' He paused. 'It doesn't sound much like kidnapping to me. But——' and he shrugged '——if you think the police will be interested I'll get them right now.' He waited for her response— imperious, tyrannical, scornful and infuriatingly right.

She didn't need to have it spelled out for her in words of one syllable. He would make himself sound like a hero with her playing the role of an ungrateful idiot. If he threw in the fact that she had been trespassing—she didn't think he would worry too much about the finer details of truth—he would probably be beatified. Given his own feast-day. With fireworks. Damn! 'Forget the police,' she muttered. 'But I don't want to rest. I just want to leave.'

'If you think that having you as a house-guest is an undiluted pleasure, Miss Nash, I have to tell you that you're mistaken. I value my privacy and you'll go the minute it's possible. We'll discuss terms after breakfast.' He turned abruptly to leave. 'I recommend a lightly boiled egg.'

'A boiled egg? I thought bread and water was the traditional prisoner's fare,' she threw after him.

His eyes darkened. Sea-green? Maybe. But what sea? The Arctic Ocean in mid-winter, perhaps? 'If that's what you want. . .' He snapped the door shut behind him.

'Wait!' But she was already talking to herself. Then in a sudden quiver of panic she ran across the room, and ignoring her painful hands almost tore at the door. But it wasn't locked. For a moment she stood there, in the open doorway, wondering whether to make a run for it down the thickly carpeted stairway. She glanced down at herself. He wasn't that careless. He didn't need a lock to keep her confined. How far would she get in a sheet, without any shoes? Without any money. She retreated into the bedroom and closed the door.

Think, Sophie, she urged herself. You need a plan. Forget the plan, she answered herself a little caustically. What you need first are some clothes. Her glance fell on the chest of drawers and, for the first time since she woke, her mouth curved in the semblance of a smile.

She gripped the brass handle of one of the drawers and pulled, biting back a cry as pain shot through her shoulder where Chay Buchanan had hauled her over the edge of the cliff. She gave up all attempts to cling on to the sheet as she eased it, recalling with a tiny spurt of anger the huge bruise that decorated her back. Monster! He hadn't needed to drag her up like that. She could have managed. Oh, really? Yes, really, she told the irritating little voice inside her head. Of course she could. But the recollection of that sickening lurch as she had missed her foothold and started to slip made her flesh rise in goose-bumps, and she shivered despite the warmth stealing in through the window as the early morning mist was burned off the sea. She had to get out of here.

She regarded the chest with loathing, but to escape she needed something to wear. This time she grasped both handles and the drawer slid open to reveal piles of beautifully ironed shirts. And this time she really smiled, with an almost irresistible curve of her lips.

She helped herself to a pale blue cotton shirt, easing her painful shoulder up to slide into the sleeve. The shirt was too big, hanging almost to her knees, but that was good. At a pinch, with a belt, she could wear it as a dress. She tried to fasten the buttons, but her fingers were stiff and painful, slowing her down, and she gave up after a couple.

She rifled through the remainder of the drawers, ignoring the ties but helping herself to a pair of thick white socks that would cushion her feet against stone. Pants? She regarded Chay Buchanan's taste for plain white American boxer shorts with dismay. They would never stay up. What she really needed was a pair of jeans and a belt. Her fingers grasped the handles of the bottom drawer as she heard his voice speaking to someone on the stairs.

She flew across the room to the bed, and as the door opened she was demure beneath the sheet. He backed in with a tray and there was just the slightest hesitation, as he regarded the shirt that now covered her anatomy, before he placed it on the table beside the bed.

'Feeling a little better?' he asked.

'Well enough to leave,' she replied brightly, ignoring

heavy, painful limbs and the overwhelming sense of weariness that her exertions had produced.

'I think that is a decision for the doctor to make.'

'Doctor?'

'He'll call in to see you later.' He regarded her thoughtfully as hope betrayed itself in her eyes. 'He's a friend, Sophie, so don't bother to bat those long eyelashes at him. He won't be impressed.'

'I've never batted an eyelash in my life!'

'No?' He sat on the edge of the bed and regarded her impassively. 'I must have mistaken the signals. I had the distinct impression that you were batting like mad yesterday morning when you asked me to sit for you.'

'That's not true!' she protested. She just hadn't been prepared for the instant response of her body to the perilous masculinity of the man, the unexpected pull of dangerous undercurrents tugging her towards something new and exciting and wonderful. She swallowed. He had seen it. Was that why his rejection had hurt so much? Because he had quite wrongly assumed that she was offering herself as a reward for his co-operation and had still said no?

He sat beside her on the bed and handed her a cup of tea, holding her clumsy fingers around it with his own. And it was still there. The urgent fire surging through her veins as he touched her. She felt the sudden start of tears to her eyes. It wasn't fair.

'Come on, Sophie, drink this,' he said. 'It'll make you feel better.'

'I doubt it,' she sniffed. It wasn't a cup of tea she needed. Her face, her whole body grew hot as she privately acknowledged that what she needed was Chay Buchanan. To be held in his arms, to. . . Oh, lord! She had always imagined herself feeling this kind of bewildering desire for a man she had fallen deeply, wonderfully in love with.

She buried her face in the cup. She hardly knew this man. And what she knew of him she didn't like. It was lust, far from pure, and shockingly simple. What she should be doing was standing under a cold shower, not lying in his bed with his warm thigh pressed against hers, separated only by the single thickness of a sheet, his hands wrapped close around hers. Why couldn't the wretched man wear a pair of trousers instead of those tailored shorts that blatantly offered his well-muscled thighs and beautifully shaped calves to her hungry eyes?

She gulped down the tea and he took the cup from her. 'Can you eat something?'

'Bread?' she asked, making an effort to keep the exchange hostile, but suddenly too weak to care much.

'The bread and water will keep,' he replied a little sharply. 'Try some toast.' She shook her head. Then wished she hadn't. 'All right. Just take these and lie down.'

She stared suspiciously at the white tablets. 'What are they?'

'Paul left them.'

'Your friendly doctor?' She withdrew slightly.

'For heaven's sake! Do you think I'm trying to drug you? He's a respected consultant with a wife and considerable quantity of children. These are just something for your headache.' He glared at her. 'You have got a headache, I hope?'

Of course she had a headache. She took the pills, swallowed them with the aid of a glass of water that he held for her as if she was an invalid. Then, as the door closed behind him, she gave up the struggle to maintain the façade of defiance, and slid down between the sheets and tried to work out just what kind of a mess Nigel's 'little favour' had got her into.

She hadn't much relished the task and had left it until the last day. . .perhaps hoping that he wouldn't be there. Nigel could hardly blame her for that.

But finally she had driven out along the coast road until she had seen the tower, just as Nigel had described it, four-square and massive, one of the many that had been built on the island to keep watch against pirates. A few in the more built-up areas had been turned into restaurants for the tourist trade. Most were abandoned. This one was surrounded by a garden.

Flowers tumbled from beds raised from the rocky ground and clambered over the walls, making the tower look more like some lost fairy-tale keep. With the impressive golden cliffs at its flanks, and the sea beyond, it had quite taken her breath away.

Close up, the tower had seemed rather more forbidding, despite the softening effect of the flowers, its entrance barricaded by a pair of heavy studded doors. But she had pinned a smile to her lips and lifted the traditional dolphin-shaped knocker.

For a long time nothing had happened. She had been trying to pluck up the courage to knock again when the door had swung open, and the figure that had filled the doorway took Sophie's breath away for the second time in less than five minutes as every cell in her body had swivelled in his direction and jumped to attention.

She had seen photographs of the man, seen him on the television, but nothing had prepared her for his overwhelming physical presence, a compelling masculinity that drew her to him like iron filings to a magnet.

'Yes?' His curt manner released her, her quick step back observed by a pair of knowing eyes that after the most cursory inspection seemed to know more about her than she did herself.

It took every shred of self-possession to keep the smile fixed to her mouth and offer her hand. 'Mr

Buchanan? Mr Chay Buchanan?' He ignored her hand, and a little self-consciously she pushed back a strand of hair that had fallen over her cheek before letting her own hand fall. 'My name is Sophie Nash.'

'Sophie Nash?' He tested the name, as if trying to recall it.

'Yes, I——'

'Maybe my memory is failing me, Miss Nash,' he interrupted without apology, 'but I don't recall an appointment with anyone of that name.' His tone invited her to prove him wrong, but with the absolute confidence of someone who knew it to be impossible.

'Well, no, I don't have an appointment,' she admitted, somewhat taken aback by this unexpected challenge.

'In that case. . .' He shrugged, stepped back and began to shut the door.

'But. . .Mr Buchanan. . . I'm. . .' Almost instinctively she reached out and held his arm. His skin was warm, very brown beneath the whiteness of her fingers, coated with silky dark hair. She snatched back her hand as if she had received an electric shock, and when she looked up again his eyes taunted her. But he didn't shut the door. 'I'm here because——'

'I know why you are here, Miss Nash,' he said, confounding her. 'Or were you deluding yourself that you were the first eager. . .fan. . .to find me? I have to admit that you are more appealing than some.' And his eyes took a slow tour of her body. 'From the top of your glossy blonde head to your pink-painted toenails,' he conceded. 'Although most have the tact to carry a copy of one of my books for me to sign. . .?' He raised a querying brow and glanced towards her bag. But she had no book to offer and silently cursed such a stupid oversight. 'That's about all I can do for you.'

She was afraid that her cheeks had gone as pink as

the despised toenails. They were certainly very hot and she would have liked to cover them with her hands, but that would be stupid. Would only draw attention to them, and to the fact that she had painted her fingernails as well. Because she had taken a great deal of trouble with her appearance.

'Wear something pretty,' Nigel had advised. 'And plenty of make-up. He can't resist a pretty face. All you'll have to do is use that winning smile of yours and you'll be in.' Well, Nigel had been wrong. It was true that she wasn't wearing much make-up. It was too warm. But the charcoal smudges on her lids emphasised the size of her large grey eyes; the mascara thickened and glossed the lashes. And she had taken infinite care to outline her lips and colour them.

She had no experience of photographing major celebrities and she had been determined to appear cool and professional. Clearly the white sleeveless jacket with its deep revers and the flirty navy and white spotted skirt had been a misjudgement in some way that totally eluded her. But it was too late to worry about that now.

'I didn't come here for your autograph, Mr Buchanan. I'm a photographer. I'm sorry if this is an awkward time. I would have telephoned to make an appointment,' she rushed on, 'but you aren't listed——'

'That,' he informed her, 'is because I don't have a telephone. It's supposed to be a strong hint that I have no wish to be disturbed by. . .casual callers.'

She was missing something. What on earth did he think she wanted? Then, with a shock, she knew. He thought she was some kind of literary groupie! It was awful. Off-the-scale embarrassment. She wanted to turn tail and run but she couldn't. Now she had found him, she had to give it everything she had got. Remembering Nigel's advice, she tried the smile. 'Mr Buchanan,' she surged on, before he could stop her or finally close the door on her. 'You've made a mistake——'

'It's you who's made the mistake, Miss Nash,' he said harshly.

'No,' she protested hotly, determined to disabuse him of his mistaken notion. 'Please listen. I simply want to take a photograph of you.' He said nothing. He didn't move. Not one muscle. It was utterly unnerving. She ran her tongue nervously over her lips as she fumbled in her bag for a card, any excuse to look away from those disturbing eyes. Her trembling fingers finally found what they were seeking and she held it out and eventually he took it, without taking his eyes from her face. 'You see?' she said, encouraging him to look at it. 'I'm a *professional* photographer.'

If she had thought that this would clear up the misunderstanding, make everything better, she had been wrong. He didn't even bother to look at her card, simply tore it in two and handed it back. 'Goodbye, Miss Nash.'

A pin-prick of anger stirred the delicate hairs on the nape of her neck, darkened her fine grey eyes, but she wasn't about to give up.

'A friend of mine is writing an article about you. . . about your work,' she rushed on quickly, before he could ask what kind of article. 'I hoped to persuade you to let me take a simple portrait. It wouldn't take long. Ten minutes. Less,' she promised. 'There's no need to change. You look fine.' Much more than fine. He presented a picture begging to be taken. His green T-shirt might be old, faded, but it was a perfect foil for his dark colouring, and the sleeves had been ripped from it, exposing strong, well-muscled arms and formidable shoulders; white tailored shorts displayed an equally powerful pair of tanned legs. He looked more like an athlete than a writer.

Still he didn't move, apparently waiting for something more. She swallowed. 'I would, of course, be prepared to pay. . .' His eyes darkened slightly. 'Whatever fee you. . .think fit.'

'Anything?' he asked, finally breaking the ominous silence.

'Anything,' she agreed recklessly, as he appeared to weaken. She wasn't about to lose him for a few pounds. Then, realising how naïve she must have sounded, she added, 'Within reason, of course.'

'And if I was. . .unreasonable?' Suddenly, without the necessity for words, she knew that this was not, had never been, a discussion about money. He had seen her reaction to him, misunderstood, thought she was actually prepared to go to bed with him to get what she wanted. Then, with a jolt, she realised that it was far worse than that. He believed that she *wanted* to go to bed with him.

Mesmerised by the idea, she remained rooted to the spot, quite unable simply to turn and walk away. Not because so much depended on getting him to sit for her. But because her legs had apparently turned to rubber. His mouth curled in a cruel parody of amusement as he made a move towards her, forcing her to look up or retreat. Sophie had no choice, and as she looked up he lifted his hand, touched the delicate hollow of her neck with the tip of one long finger, his brows lifting just a fraction as she felt the shock start through her body.

'Well, well,' he murmured. 'Such flattering eagerness.' Then, as his eyes held her fixed like a rabbit mesmerised by the headlights of an oncoming car, his finger traced the line of her breastbone with agonising slowness, until it came to rest against the white linen where it crossed between her breasts. Her lips parted on a sharp, anguished breath as her nipples tightened against the cloth.

'Nice try, Miss Nash. But your friend should have warned you that I don't talk to reporters or photographers. No matter how appealing the inducement.'

With a superhuman effort she raised her hand to slap away the fingers that lingered against the soft swell of her breast. 'How dare you?' she croaked.

'Dare?' He had ignored the slap, but now he withdrew his hand and she could breathe again. Just. 'For my privacy I would dare a very great deal. I give you fair warning, Miss Sophie Nash, that if I find you anywhere near my home with a camera in your possession, you'll discover that the dungeon is still a working feature. And that's where you'll remain until I decide otherwise.'

Now, lying in his bed, Sophie almost jumped again as she recalled the slam of the great front door. She knew she had to escape. Get away from this insufferable man as quickly as possible. A yawn caught her by surprise and her lids, suddenly unbearably heavy, drifted shut. It was important. But she would just have a little sleep first.

CHAPTER THREE

SOPHIE woke, stretched, regarded her unconventional sleeping wear with a slight frown and pulled herself upright, wincing as the aches immediately re-established themselves, to confront a pair of dark, inquisitive eyes regarding her with open curiosity. The same dark eyes that had spotted the flash of her lens against the sun. They belonged to a boy of about five or six years of age who was sitting cross-legged at the end of the bed.

'Hello,' she said.

He leaned forward a little, excitement barely contained. 'What was it like?' he asked.

'I'm sorry?'

'On the cliff.' He flung an arm in that general direction.

'Oh.' She wondered what he expected. Breathless excitement and danger? The truth would probably be best. 'It was hot and dusty,' she offered, and hid a smile at his open scorn. 'And very. . .frightening.'

'I wouldn't be frightened,' he said, clearly dismissing her fears as something to be expected of a woman. 'I'm going to climb it. . .one day. All the way.'

The thought made her feel suddenly queasy. 'Well, make sure you take a rope,' she advised.

'You didn't,' he pointed out.

'I was stupid. Your father had to rescue me.'

He regarded her with something like pity. 'But you're a girl.'

She could offer no argument to that. Male chauvinism lives, she thought, passed down from father to son. 'What's your name?'

'Tom! What are you doing in here?' The boy scrambled off the bed guiltily. 'I told you to leave Miss Nash alone.'

'I didn't wake her up, Papa. She did it all by herself. Didn't you?' He appealed to Sophie.

'All by myself,' she agreed. 'He didn't disturb me. Really.'

Chay Buchanan was not to be so easily placated. 'Go and have your tea. Theresa is waiting for you.'

Tom gave her an uncertain little smile, bravado extinguished. 'Sorry,' he muttered.

'Don't be, Tom. Enjoy your tea.' She watched the door close beind him with regret as she was forced instead to confront his stony-faced father, who leaned towards her and grasped her arm.

'What were you asking him?' There was no mistaking the raw anger in his voice, his face, the way his fingers bit into the soft flesh.

'I didn't ask him anything. Despite your low opinion of me, I am not in the habit of interrogating children.'

'You're suggesting that such a thing would be beneath you?' he demanded, disbelief stamped in every line of his face.

She glared at him. 'I'm not suggesting it,' she retorted coldly. 'I'm telling it like it is.' For a moment their eyes clashed.

'So what were you talking about?' The fingers bit deeper and she tried not to wince visibly.

'He. . .he asked me about the cliff.'

'The cliff?' He paled visibly. 'What did he ask you?' There was an urgency about him that intrigued her, despite her attempt to hold herself apart. He gave her a little shake. 'What did you tell him?'

'He just asked what it was like. I told him it was frightening and that I had been stupid. . .'

'And?'

'He took the view that I was feeble because I was a girl.' She paused, then added, because she thought he should know, 'He said he was going to climb it himself one day.'

'Damn you,' he said, through tight lips.

'Frankly, Mr Buchanan, I don't think it had anything to do with me. But perhaps some simple lessons in rock-climbing would be a wise precaution,' she advised, with feeling. 'Let him have a taste of the pain as well as the excitement.'

He swept his hand through a dark lock of hair that had fallen over his forehead. 'No.' A muscle was working furiously at his mouth. 'He's not going anywhere near that damned cliff.' He glared down at her. 'I don't have to ask how you are,' he snapped. 'Obviously a great deal better.'

'Yes,' she replied. And some small devil prompted her to add a gentle, 'Thank you for asking.' It brought her a sharp look. 'Quite well enough to leave.'

'You'll leave when it suits me, Miss Nash. In the meantime you'll stay where you are until Paul has checked you over. Don't say anything stupid to him,' he warned.

Stupid? Like what? Help me, I'm being held prisoner? She managed a sweetly insincere smile. 'What could I say? You're a hero. A positive saint——'

'Stop it!' She shrugged and subsided against the bed. He leaned over her and grasped her chin, forcing her to look into his eyes. 'Behave yourself, Sophie Nash. Or I'm warning you, you'll never see your precious films again. Is that quite clear?'

Oh, wouldn't it be utter bliss to tell him to take her films and go to hell with them? The temptation was almost overwhelming. But she would have to do the work again, at her own expense. And he didn't only have her films. He had her camera. And there was Jennie. She hadn't quite given up on the chance that she might yet snatch her films and run. 'Quite clear,' she said demurely.

For a moment he scrutinised her face, as if not quite believing in such a quick capitulation, and she forced herself to meet his disquieting gaze head-on and ignore the sudden quickening of her pulse, the intoxicating sense of her own fragility as she was confronted by the man's almost barbaric magnetism.

Finally, he released her, but the imprint of his fingers remained burned into her face. She was breathless, her pulse jumping, not quite in control. Unlike her gaoler, who was regarding her without any trace of emotion to disturb his arrogant features. 'You must be hungry,' he said prosaically, as if to confirm her opinion. 'When Paul's finished with you, come downstairs for supper. Theresa's made you some soup.'

She plucked at the shirt she was wearing. 'Could I have some clothes?'

'Not for the moment. Not until I've decided what to do with you.' He regarded her steadily. 'You seem to be pretty resourceful. I'm sure you'll manage.'

A tap on the door interrupted the flash of annoyance that sparked her eyes, threatening to erupt and undo all her hard-won attempts to be civil to the man. Chay rose from the bed and admitted the slight figure of the doctor.

'Don't take her blood pressure, Paul,' he warned as he turned to leave. 'I have the feeling that it will blow your machine.'

But the doctor did not take the warning seriously. He checked her eyes, listened to her chest, took the dangerous blood pressure and declared it to be fine, delicately probed her shoulder and finally examined her hands.

'Take it easy for a few days, Miss Nash,' he finally advised her. 'Get plenty of sleep and you will be fine.' He rose. 'I'll look in again tomorrow, but I hope to find you outside, sitting in the shade.' He paused. 'And stay away from cliffs in future. Particularly that one.'

'Why?'

Dr Paul Manduca regarded his patient thoughtfully. 'Some questions, Miss Nash, are better not asked.' He picked up his bag. 'I'll see you again tomorrow. Good evening.'

Evening? This time she didn't even bother to query the time. Chay Buchanan had invited her downstairs for supper. If she was hungry. By her somewhat unreliable reckoning it must be at least thirty hours since she had eaten an apple, something to do to break the boredom of the endless wait as she had hoped that Chay Buchanan would take a swim. She had eaten it with the thoughtlessness of someone who knew her next meal would only be an hour or two away. If she was hungry? She swung her legs from the bed. She was ravenous. But before she left this room she had to make herself decent.

She washed, used his comb to disentangle her hair painfully, then quite shamelessly helped herself to a fresh white shirt. Her fingers were hurting less and she made herself fasten all but the top two buttons. Then she tackled the bottom drawer. But there were no jeans. Just sweaters and shorts.

She held a pair of navy shorts against herself. Not bad. She pulled them on, but the minute she let go they fell about her ankles. She glared at them. She wasn't about to be beaten by a pair of shorts. All she needed was something to hold them up with. A tie. She found the drawer with the socks and ties and quickly threaded one tie through the loops and knotted it firmly in place around her waist. Then she took another, rather beautiful silk tie in deep red and tied it over the shirt, grinning appreciatively at her reflection in the bathroom mirror. She decided against the socks. She had the feeling they would rather spoil the effect.

She opened the bedroom door and jumped, confronted with the tower's disturbing inhabitant. But she didn't miss the glitter of a pair of vivid eyes as he absorbed her attempt at sartorial elegance, or the deepening of the lines etched into his cheeks.

'You took so long, I thought that something must be wrong.'

'Wrong? Whatever could be wrong, Mr Buchanan?' she enquired smoothly. 'I was simply taking my time deciding what to wear.'

'It's an interesting combination.' He walked around her, inspecting the result of her raid on his wardrobe. 'In fact, it's oddly sexy.' His eyes met her furious glance. 'But I imagine it was your sex appeal, rather than your skill with a camera, that won you this particular assignment.'

Sex appeal? The idea was so alien that she was for once left without a reply. She had certainly taken Nigel's advice and tried to look. . .tempting. . .when she had set out to persuade Chay Buchanan to let her take his photograph. That she might have succeeded was disturbing, especially as she was now quite at the mercy of her intended victim.

Sophie sat back and sighed with contentment after eating her fill of a thick vegetable soup in the style of minestrone, but with beans and pork added to it. 'That was wonderful, Theresa,' she said, and added two of the few Maltese words she had learned. '*Grazzi, hafna.*' The middle-aged woman who kept house for

Chay Buchanan beamed briefly, before turning on him to launch into a rapid speech in her native tongue. Then she flounced back into the kitchen with the dishes. Sophie watched her go and then turned to Chay. 'What was all that about?' she asked.

'Theresa is rather old-fashioned. She does not think it quite "proper" for a young lady to be wearing clothes that belong to a man. Especially a man she doesn't know.'

Sophie, hunger assuaged by Theresa's excellent cooking, was feeling considerably mellower. 'I agree with her,' she said, quite seriously, 'but since the alternative was the sheet. . .' She left the sentence unfinished, tucking away the knowledge that she might have an ally of sorts in Chay's housekeeper.

For a moment his eyes lingered on the opening of his shirt at her throat and it took all her self-possession to restrain herself from clutching it together. After what seemed an eternity he raised his eyes to hers. 'There was nothing wrong with the sheet,' he said.

'You weren't wearing it,' she replied crisply. 'And I think Theresa has been scandalised more than enough for one day.' She thought his lips twitched slightly as he contemplated that fierce lady's likely reaction to the sight of Sophie wrapped in a sheet that refused to stay put. Indignant that he should find amusement in her predicament she snapped, 'You might as well let me have my own clothes, Mr Buchanan, since, as you took such gratification in pointing out, I'm not going anywhere without my films or my camera.' She paused. 'Assuming, of course, that you haven't already done what you threatened and flung them into the sea.' And she held her breath, half expecting him to say that he had.

But he didn't. He didn't mention them at all. 'Theresa has made up the guest-room for you. You'll

find your clothes have been unpacked and put away.'
He stood up. 'We'll have coffee in the living-room,' he
said, taking her arm to help her to her feet.

'What a pity she's gone to so much trouble,' she
said, in an effort to provoke him, to ignore the warm
touch of his fingers at her elbow, 'I'll only have to
repack them all.' He refused to rise. Common sense
told her to leave it. But where Chay Buchanan was
concerned she seemed to have no sense at all, common
or otherwise. 'And my camera bag?' she demanded. 'Is
that all laid out and ready for me as well?' Then she
held her breath, waiting for him to explode. But he
merely glanced down at her.

'No, Sophie. It isn't. But I haven't flung your camera
into the sea. It's quite safe for the time being.' He
opened one of a pair of doors and ushered her into a
room similar in size and shape to his bedroom. Perhaps
it was slightly larger, thirty or forty feet long, but the
evening had closed in and the soft illumination from
the lamp on a table didn't reach that far. 'Sit down.'
He waved her to a chair. 'You'd better make yourself
at home.'

Home! Of all the nerve. . . And she'd sit when she
was good and ready; she had far more important things
on her mind than sitting down. 'What about my films?'
she demanded. He hadn't mentioned them and she
feared the worst.

'Black or white?' he responded aggravatingly, as he
lifted the heavy silver coffee-pot.

'Neither—they were colour transparencies,' she
snapped.

'So they were.' He relented a little as he saw dismay
cloud her eyes. 'They still are. For the moment. Sit
down, Sophie.'

She remained where she was. 'What are you going
to do with them?' she insisted.

He put down the coffee-pot and moved towards her with an air of purpose. Before she realised what he was about to do, could utter a protest, he had scooped her up into his arms and carried her towards a large squashy leather chair and dumped her in it. The moment was brief, over almost before she could register the pleasurable warmth of his bare arm against the back of her knees, the thud of his heartbeat as, for a second or two, her cheek had been pressed against the broad expanse of his chest.

Instinctively she drew her knees to her chin and curled up in a self-protective attitude. She wasn't used to a man being able to light her up with nothing more than a touch, a look. She didn't like the power it gave him. It frightened her. But she said nothing. She'd got the message loud and clear. Do as she was told. Sophie hid her pique under lowered lids as he returned to the coffee-pot.

'Black or white?' He repeated the question as if nothing unusual had happened. Her hands curled into tight, painful fists. Nothing *had* happened. Only in her head.

'White, please,' she murmured, her voice meekly obedient, and received a sharp look for her trouble as he passed her a cup.

Sophie sipped her coffee, trying to disregard the sense of the absurd, the complete unreality of her situation, as she faced him from across the wide expanse of a stone hearth. She was a grown woman, with a career and a growing respect in her profession, behaving just like a good little girl, waiting to be told what he had decided to do with her property. Worse. She was being held a virtual prisoner by the kind of man mothers warned their daughters about. Not that she had needed warning. She had recognised the danger signals the moment those knowing eyes had regarded her from his threshold.

Oh? that inner voice queried, with irritating percipience. So why didn't you run away when you had the chance? So, why *hadn't* she? Heaven knew that he had warned her in no uncertain terms to stay away from him.

He was sitting opposite her, relaxed, totally at ease, his long legs stretched out before him on a worn Persian carpet, balancing a coffee-cup in one hand, watching her from beneath heavy-lidded eyes. She blinked. It had been worth the risk. It was still worth any risk.

'Well?' she demanded, her voice thick with tension. 'Don't keep me in suspense any longer, Mr Buchanan. What are you going to do with the films?'

'That's rather up to you, Miss Sophie Nash,' he said softly.

She regarded him with utter disbelief, but he was apparently waiting for some response. She made a good attempt at a casual shrug. 'Well, that's easy,' she said. 'Just hand them over and I'll be on my way.'

'I'm sure even you can't believe it would be quite that easy.' He regarded her steadily for a moment. 'You have only two choices. And I'm being generous.'

'I'm glad you think so.'

'The first,' he continued, as if she had not spoken, 'is simply to destroy the lot. I don't think anyone would blame me.'

'*I* would blame you. In fact, Mr Buchanan, I should be very unhappy,' she pointed out.

'Your happiness is neither here nor there. Right now the only thing I care about is my privacy.'

'Why?' she demanded.

'Why not?' he returned with infuriating urbanity. 'Or maybe you would enjoy having a long-lens camera pointed at you from some hidden vantage point?

Perhaps when you were in the bath? Or sunbathing topless in the garden? And the results published in the newspaper?'

'I've never sunbathed topless in my life,' she protested, then blushed as one dark brow rose askance at her vehemence. 'Besides, no one would print it,' she continued defiantly. 'I'm not——' She stopped, suddenly realising where this was leading.

'You are not famous?' he suggested. 'Should that matter?'

'Maybe not,' she said, unable to stop herself squirming a little, letting her eyes drop from his penetrating gaze. 'But it does.'

'Yes, it does,' he agreed. 'So I made a conscious decision to stop being famous. I intend to keep it that way.' The question, Why? sprang to her lips once more, but this time she didn't let it beyond them. 'And for goodness' sake call me Chay,' he said. 'Mr Buchanan makes me feel about ninety.'

She recalled the sight of his sleekly muscled body as it had curved into the water. There was nothing remotely old about Chay Buchanan. He was a man at the peak of his power, the peak of his life. So what was he doing here, living alone with a small boy? Had his wife deserted him? Broken his heart? Was that the story Nigel was going to write? She found that she wanted to know, but a direct question was unlikely to produce an answer. 'You might as well be,' she said casually, although her heart was thumping furiously. 'After all, you've retired. Given up on life. . .just for the sake of a little privacy.'

'Who says I've retired?' The cool voice rippled with the warning that she was treading thin ice. She chose to ignore it.

'You haven't written anything in years, you've hidden yourself away in this place. You've simply

stepped off the end of the world and stopped living.'
She challenged him to deny it.

'And you're anxious to remind me of what I'm
missing?' he retaliated smoothly, his eyes glittering.
For a moment she took on the anger, met him head-on
while her pulse-rate accelerated alarmingly. Then she
found herself staring at her battered hands, her breathing too rapid for comfort. This was a man, she discovered, that you challenged at your peril. 'No? Then
shall we stick to the matter in hand?'

She swallowed hard. 'I believe I had two choices?
What was the second?'

He didn't answer, but stood up and fetched her
camera bag from the dim recesses at the far end of the
room. When he dropped it carelessly on the table in
front of her she reached out, wanting to grab it close,
protect it from him. But his strong fingers fastened
about her wrist and stayed the anxious movement.

Then he folded the long length of his body until his
eyes were on a level with hers and, poised on his toes
beside her chair, he held her, dominated her with the
careless arrogance of a man who knew he was invin-
cible. 'As I said, we destroy the films now, Sophie. All
of them.' He ignored her sharp protest and with his
free hand flipped the bag open and took one out. 'It's
quite simple.' The pad of his thumb whitened against
the cassette and Sophie physically jumped as the film
burst free of its confinement and spewed into her lap.
Utterly ruined. She let out a low groan. All that work
for nothing. Unmoved by her dismay, he picked up
another cassette. 'That was the one I took from your
pocket,' he reassured her. 'This one might be anything.' His hand tightened over the spool of film.

'No!' Her hand flew to rescue her precious film, but
his fist tightened about it.

'Sure?' he demanded.

She swallowed. 'You've destroyed the film I took of you. There's no need to ruin the rest.'

He regarded her with something like pity. 'I have destroyed *one* of the films you took of me.'

'I only took one,' she said, but perhaps just a little too quickly.

'Sophie, Sophie,' he said, remonstrating softly. 'I can understand your eagerness to impress me with your probity. Doubtless a considerable amount of money rides on your being able to get away with your pictures. But I'm afraid that your record-keeping is too thorough.' He tossed the film back in the bag and, releasing her wrist, he produced a small hard-bound notebook from its interior. 'There are fifty-seven films listed in this little red book of yours. You've had a busy week.' He turned the pages, scanning her entries. 'Hotels, villas, a holiday village,' he said, looking up. 'I'm glad you've found time for a little culture too. Ancient sites, museums, Mosta Dom,' he listed as he flicked through the pages. 'Then there was the obligatory trip to Gozo to see the lace-makers and Calypso's cave. And we mustn't forget the perennial favourites. The Blue Grotto, a variety of picturesque harbours, the *dghajsa*-man and the pleasures of the *karrozzin* ride. Everything, in fact, that the tourist would want to see in Malta. All annotated with precision.'

'Of course,' she agreed. 'I always make notes as I take photographs. So?'

'So?' he echoed mockingly. 'There are *fifty-nine* films in your bag, Sophie. Plus the one I took from your shirt-pocket. There appear to be not one, but two cuckoos in the nest.'

'Oh!' The sound rushed from her in a little sigh.

Satisfied that he had her full attention, he continued. 'Of course, it may be that you simply forgot to record them?' He waited for her to confirm that this was the case. But she didn't bother. She knew he wouldn't believe her.

'No. I didn't forget.'

'No. You simply didn't have time to record the last three films, did you, Sophie?' He flung the notebook on the table and stood up. 'You were too busy trying to kill yourself in your hurry to get away with your ill-gotten gains.'

She ignored this, unwilling to think about what had happened. 'Your first offer of choice was destruction. What is the second?'

He stared down at the bag of films. 'We could have them processed.'

'Processed?' she repeated with astonishment. But a little spark of hope kindled in her breast. 'And you would keep the photographs I took of you? That's very generous of you, Mr. . .Chay.' And she managed what she hoped was a truly grateful smile.

'Yes,' he agreed, his own smile mocking her. 'In the circumstances, I think it is.'

'Of course,' she said slowly, 'you may not realise that they will have to go to Kodak in Paris. It will take a few days.'

'To Paris?' he asked with a slight frown. 'Why?'

Because Kodak would despatch the processed transparencies to their London office to await her collection, as they always did, no matter where in the world they were sent from. She would still have two rolls of film. It took iron control to hide her triumph. Any sense of guilt about her long-distance photography had rapidly dissipated in the heat of his aggression. 'Because it's professional film. For professional reproduction,' she said seriously. 'I'm afraid the quality control at some backstreet chemist shop in Sliema won't quite do.'

He smiled back. At least, his mouth smiled. His eyes

were not joining in. 'You, of course, will stay here until they return.'

Her eyes widened. She hadn't expected that. But then she shrugged, as if it didn't matter. Once they were out of his hands she would surely find some means of escape, but it wouldn't do to concede too quickly. 'Surely. . .there's no need. I'll give you my address,' she offered, diplomatically choosing to overlook the fact that, since he had all her belongings, he certainly already knew her address. 'You can just send on anything that doesn't include you.'

His eyes narrowed. 'You're very trusting.'

'Shouldn't I be? You wouldn't keep them, would you?' she asked.

'You'll never know, Sophie, because you are going to stay here, under close supervision, until they return.'

'As your prisoner?' she demanded.

His eyes darkened. 'I could still be tempted simply to trash the lot right now.' His hand hovered over the bag.

'No.' She leapt to her feet, reaching out a protective hand to grasp his wrist before he could carry out his threat. 'You. . . You'd better show me to your dungeon.'

His mouth straightened in a smile. Not a very big smile. Just horribly self-satisfied. 'Forget about the dungeon, Sophie. I have something far more entertaining in mind.'

She snatched her hand away from his wrist as if burned, eyes wide as her thoughts immediately flew to his huge bed on the floor above. Surely he didn't mean. . .? 'Can't sing, can't dance. . .' she almost croaked.

'No?' he asked, as if he didn't quite believe her. 'But then I'm not looking for a cabaret act. How are you in the kitchen, Sophie?'

'The kitchen?' she repeated, as if the word was strange to her. Not the bedroom?

'Yes,' he confirmed, 'the kitchen. Theresa has asked for a few days' holiday. I think it would be a happy solution all round if you were to take her place for a week. A small repayment for all the bother you have caused.'

'You mean, stay here alone with you?' she asked, horrified at the prospect.

He seemed to find her response amusing. 'Not quite alone. There's Tom.'

'Tom? I don't think he would make a very satisfactory chaperon.'

'You want a chaperon? A modern young woman who would risk her life to get a scoop? Come along, Miss Nash, surely you're not afraid?' His eyes offered her a dare. 'I've stepped off the world, remember? Retired from life. What kind of a threat can I possibly pose?'

She didn't want to consider the threat he represented, but was prepared to concede for the first time in her life that mothers knew a thing or two. 'Just how old are you?' she asked. 'As a matter of interest.'

'As a matter of interest?' He regarded her thoughtfully. 'Thirty. . .something.'

Four? Five? No more. 'That old?' she asked, her heart beating ridiculously fast. She made a play of looking around, then quite deliberately raised a pair of grave grey eyes to meet the ocean depths of his. 'So? Where do you keep your walking-frame?'

'You, Sophie Nash,' he said, grasping her shoulders with a fierceness which warned her that resistance was pointless, 'are a very foolish, very impertinent young woman. And quite definitely in need of a lesson in respect when speaking to your elders. I ought to put you over my knee and spank you, right now!'

'Do you think you could manage it?' she persisted in defiance.

'You choose to live dangerously, Miss Nash,' he ground out. 'But you've got enough bruises for one day.' He jerked her towards him. 'Consider this a down payment.'

CHAPTER FOUR

SOPHIE'S instinctive protest played straight into his hands, but by the time she realised that it was too late to clamp her mouth shut. He was quite unmoved by her attempts to free herself, carelessly releasing one shoulder before capturing her waist to pull her close against the warmth of his body, force her to acknowledge his dominance.

She immediately stopped struggling. It didn't need the urgent flicker of response from her own body to warn her that, clamped against his hard thighs, struggling would be foolhardy in the extreme. Instead she remained perfectly still. Determinedly unresponsive. Then an exquisite shiver ran through her body as it refused to co-operate with her brain. No one could remain unresponsive to such a man.

His mouth was a revelation. She had known it would be. Anger had not disguised the well-cut sensuality of a full lower lip that, without haste, was now demolishing the few shreds of self-possession she had managed to cling to.

He had said she should be taught a lesson and she had expected a hard, bruising kiss. Easy to resist. He knew that as well as she did. Chay Buchanan was too subtle for such caveman tactics. Instead the delicate, teasing caresses of his mouth, the heady pressure of his body against hers, were the kindling that lit a fire in her veins; his lips and tongue were the fan to her desire, until it was she who was kissing him, tempting him, demanding more. And it was Chay Buchanan who broke away, his eyes unreadable in the lamplight.

'Now, Miss Nash,' he demanded, 'would you care to repeat that remark about a walking-frame?'

She gasped, pulled away from him. While she had been lost to the world, cloud-waltzing on desire, he had been intent upon simply making a point, humiliating her. Some lesson! One that she would be slow to forget. She would hang on to her temper, stow her pride in the attic and remember the old adage—don't get mad, get even. Somehow, some way, she would make him pay for that.

And, with that silent promise of retribution, she lifted her chin, pinned a smile to her mouth and turned to face him, only the little black flecks that darkened her irises a betrayal of her true state of mind for those lucky enough to interpret the signals and run for cover.

'I withdraw it unreservedly, Mr Buchanan. Despite being thirty——' and she shrugged slightly '—something, you are clearly still a little way short of your dotage. Now, shall we pack up the film? Then perhaps you would be kind enough to point me in the direction of the servants' quarters?' He regarded her steadily, almost, she thought, with a touch of grudging appreciation for her acting ability. What had he expected? Hysterics? It was as well he couldn't see behind her cool façade to the seething mass of emotions that were churning around her brain and sending confused signals sparking through her body. Hysterics were nothing to what she felt like throwing.

'I'll see to the films in the morning,' he assured her. 'I think perhaps you've had enough for your first time out of bed.'

More than enough. More than enough of Chay Buchanan to last a lifetime. 'I've been in bed all day,' she reminded him. 'I'm not tired.' There was something important that she had to do. Casually, she took a roll of tiny sticky labels from her bag and began to fasten one to each of the films with fingers that trembled just a little.

'What are you doing?'

She looked up with what she hoped was nonchalance. 'Just indentifying the films with my account number.' She forced her lips to offer a smile. A very little smile. 'I can hardly expect you to pay for the processing.'

His eyes narrowed slightly as he stared at the bag. 'Leave it now. If you're not tired you might as well come out on to the terrace and have some fresh air.'

She hesitated for just a second before dropping the film back in the bag. If she protested, he would become suspicious. 'That would be. . .lovely.'

He opened the tall French windows and warm, moist air, laden with the scent of the sea, rushed to meet them. She took a deep breath and devoured the panorama spread before her. The little island of Comino was almost close enough to touch, and beyond that the light-strewn shape of Gozo, where the enchantress Calypso imprisoned Odysseus for seven long years, glittered in the dark sweep of the sea. 'Lord, but this is a beautiful spot,' she murmured.

'I thought you disapproved.'

'Disapproved? Why should I do that?' She glanced at him. 'This is a retreat. A place to go when you want to get away from everything.' She turned back to the sea. 'Not a place to live, though, unless you're a lotus-eater.'

'And is that what you think I am?'

No, she didn't think that. She didn't think that Chay Buchanan was idle, or even particularly happy in his island paradise. But she didn't say so. 'I can see the temptation,' she said, with apparent sympathy. 'The danger is that, like poor old Odysseus, you won't be able to escape. It's too easy just to stay put.' She turned to him. 'Why did you stop writing, Chay? What are you hiding from?'

His eyes flashed a warning. 'Surely your commissioning editor gave you the smallest hint?'

Commissioning editor? She wanted to laugh at the idea. Or cry. Nigel was nothing more than a hack freelance journalist. But she wasn't about to tell Chay that. 'Why don't you give me your side of the story?' she suggested.

'Nice try, Sophie, but, despite the fact that for the moment I choose not to be published, I write every day of my life, and if I were hiding I promise you would never have found me. So you'll just have to make it up as you go along. That's the usual method, so it shouldn't be difficult.'

'I wouldn't know; I don't make up anything. I just take the pictures.' Damn! That had come out all wrong. As if she spent her life hiding in corners and taking photographs of reluctant celebrities. 'I just take pictures,' she corrected herself.

His cynical smile suggested that he was not convinced. 'Would you like a drink? A small brandy, perhaps?'

'Thank you,' she said quickly, glad of any change of subject.

'Sit over there and I'll fetch it.'

He pointed her in the direction of the kind of swinging garden seat that had featured heavily in American romantic comedy movies in the late fifties and early sixties. The sort where a tremulous virgin, trying to prove how sophisticated she was, came perilously close to being seduced by a wicked older man, usually with the assistance of a large glass of brandy, only to be rescued by the hero in the nick of time.

Chay bent over her and offered a beautiful crystal goblet in which a small amount of amber liquid reposed. She stared at it for a moment, then glanced up at him, trying to read his expression in the dim light. Who would rescue her, she wondered, if Chay Buchanan decided to take advantage of the weakness she had already betrayed?

She took the glass, jumping nervously as her fingers brushed his, and he stretched himself alongside her, his arm along her shoulders, and began to rock the chair, very slowly. 'Who are you working for, Sophie?'

'What?' His question had been so far from her own disturbing train of thought that she jumped.

'It was a perfectly simple question.'

'Yes, of course it was.' She took a ragged breath. 'Island Holidays. I did the Canaries for them during the winter. Apparently they were pleased enough with the result to give me Sicily and Malta this year.'

'That's very interesting. Now perhaps you would be kind enough to answer my question.'

'But——'

'Sophie!' he warned.

'I'm not employed by anyone,' she said, abruptly conceding defeat.

'You were simply doing a little freelancing on your own account?'

What could she say? She glanced at him. Could he possibly understand why she had been driven to such desperate measures.? She shivered a little. Of course not. What could a man like him know of such things? But if she lied, said she was doing it for herself, for what she could get, it would confirm his view that she was someone who robbed people of their privacy for money. She discovered that she didn't want him to think that badly of her.

'A friend asked me to try and get a picture of you while I was in Malta. I told you, he's writing an article about you. It was simply a. . .favour. I won't be paid.'

'And how far would you have gone,' he drawled, 'for a favour?'

'How far?'

His fingers trailed beneath the collar of her shirt and began to stroke the nape of her neck. She tensed and tried to move, to escape, but he was too quick, capturing her throat with his free hand, cupping it in his palm, tilting her head back until she was staring up into his eyes. 'All the way?' His thumb brushed lightly across her lips.

'No!' She pushed him away.

He laughed softly but made no attempt to hold her. 'Do you really expect me to believe that?'

Something snapped. 'I don't care whether you believe it or not.' She put the glass on a small table and tried to stand up, but the treacherous swing of the chair caught her off-balance and she was thrown back against him. He caught her round the waist, pulling her down on to his lap, his eyes dark as he searched her face.

'He must be a very special friend, if you're prepared to risk so much—even your life—to please him.'

'I didn't. . .' she protested, then, catching his tormenting eye, she lifted her shoulders in a tiny shrug. 'I didn't mean to.' He raised a disconcerting brow and she blushed furiously as she realised that her denial fitted both scenarios. But maybe she should emphasise her friendship with Nigel. Although heaven knew that nothing could have been further from the truth, it might be wise to suggest that there was someone out there to worry about her. 'Yes, if you must know. Nigel is very special. Now, will you let me go?' She tried to pull free.

'Your lover?' he persisted.

'How dare you?'

His grip at her waist tightened warningly. 'The

prisoner must expect a certain amount of interrogation. Tell me about him,' he insisted.

But she didn't want to talk about Nigel. She thrust her hands towards him. 'Here. If you want my secrets, you'll have to use thumb-screws. I'm sure you must have a pair tucked away in your dungeon.'

If she had hoped to make him angry, she failed. He took one of her hands in his, turned it over. 'I think not. Your hands have suffered quite enough.' He lifted it to his lips and kissed the pad of her thumb. The warmth of his mouth sent a dangerous charge of longing surging crazily through her body, and she snatched her hand away as if stung. He grinned, quite suddenly, taking her quite by surprise. 'And I don't really think I'd need to employ torture if I wanted to learn your secrets, Sophie. Do you?'

'I don't know what you mean,' she protested, making a further unsuccessful effort to pull free of his grasp, the infuriating swing of the chair simply rocking her back against his chest.

'Of course you do, Sophie,' he murmured. 'Or you wouldn't be quite so anxious to escape.'

'Can't you stop this thing?' she demanded.

'Whenever I want. But I'm perfectly happy for the moment.' He shifted slightly, so that her head somehow became cradled in the hollow of his shoulder and there was nothing to struggle against. Instead she held herself as rigid as she could.

But the gentle rocking of the seat, the warmth of the brandy inside her, the steady thud of his heartbeat beneath her cheek was a bewitching combination. She could well understand any *ingénue* succumbing without a struggle to such an assault on her senses. The wonder of it was that she should be grateful to be rescued by some priggish young man.

She started. What on earth was she thinking? What was she doing, lying back in the arms of the enemy?

She cleared her throat. 'I seem to be falling asleep. Perhaps I'd better go to bed after all.' She tried to move, but his arm pinioned her against his chest.

'Just one thing before you go, Sophie.'

'Yes?' she queried, suspicious of the velvet-smooth drawl to his voice.

'Tell me what happened to the films you took in Sicily.'

She opened her eyes wide and stared at him. 'Sicily?' she repeated as her mind clicked into overdrive, playing for time in which to think.

'You were commissioned to take photographs in Sicily for Island Holidays. Didn't you say so?'

'Did I?' she asked. Would he believe her if she said she was on her way there next? A small ray of hope offered the possibility of escape. If she could convince him that she was expected there tomorrow. . .that if she didn't arrive people would worry and raise the alarm, search for her. . . Then she met a pair of hard eyes, gleaming in the darkness, and hope died. Of course not. He had her airline ticket. He knew perfectly well that she had already been there.

'Well?'

'I sent them to Paris before I left Palermo.'

'I see. And what happens to them after that?' She had the uncomfortable feeling that he knew very well what happened to them. That all the time he had been playing with her.

'They're sent back, of course.'

'Of course,' he agreed. 'But not to Sicily.'

She gave a small laugh. 'Well, no.'

'Well, no,' he repeated, and offered a nasty little parody of her laugh. But he wasn't amused. And when he spoke again his voice had lost its velvet caress. It struck at her like flint against steel. 'They get returned in accordance with your standing instructions, don't they? Straight back to base.' He stood up abruptly and dumped her on her feet. 'Your little labels have been bothering me, Sophie. But now I see the point. Very clever. Too clever by half. I think I'd better take you up to your room right now, before I change my mind about the dungeon.'

'Frankly, Mr Buchanan,' she declared furiously, 'I'd prefer the dungeon. At least then we could forget this pretence of civilised behaviour!'

'You don't know what the word means,' he growled. 'In the circumstances I've behaved with wholly admirable restraint!'

'Admirable restraint?' she gasped. 'Words fail me.'

'Now that would make a pleasant change,' he said. 'But I don't think I'll hold my breath.'

'You are truly the rudest, most infuriating and downright obnoxious man it has ever been my misfortune to meet,' she declared fervently, close to tears but determined that he shouldn't see.

'Am I? Well, it's a misfortune you brought entirely upon yourself. And I think you've pushed your luck quite far enough for one day.'

'Oh? Have I, indeed? And what about you? Aren't you just a little bit afraid that I'll tell everyone exactly what you've done, when you do eventually let me go?' She brushed aside his attempt to interrupt. 'And I don't mean the police,' she rushed on, 'I'm talking about the newspapers.'

'You don't come out of the encounter exactly covered with roses,' he retaliated harshly.

'No?' She scowled at him. 'Well, if I were the sort of person you seem to think I am, Chay Buchanan, would I actually *care*?' She made a gesture with her hands, indicating a banner. '"Bestselling author held me captive".' She paused briefly, then repeated the gesture. '"I was Chay Buchanan's slave". Or, what about——' She raised her hands once more, but this time he caught her wrists in a vice-like grip.

'Enough!'

'You'd be famous enough then,' she advised him recklessly. 'Your precious privacy wouldn't stand a chance. . .'

Her voice trailed away as angry eyes compelled her to silence. 'That was a mistake, Sophie,' he said, his voice like chips of ice in her veins. 'A very big mistake. I'm afraid you're going to have to stay here for rather longer than I had anticipated.'

'What do you mean longer. . .? You can't——'

'Can't I? Who's to stop me?' She swallowed nervously as his ransacking glance pinned her helpless to the spot and, releasing her wrists, he grasped a handful of her long fair hair to twist about his fist. 'I could keep you prisoner at the top of my tower for so long that, like Rapunzel, you'd have to let down your long hair and hope that some passing sailor would be tempted to climb it and set you free.'

Her mouth dried. 'You're crazy!'

'Am I?' He tightened his grip and began to lead her, using her hair as a halter, towards the tower, and she had little choice other than to follow him like an obedient spaniel as he tugged sharply at her scalp.

'What are you going to do with me?' she demanded, still defiant despite the quiver of anxiety which told her that she had, indeed, gone too far. Much too far.

His glance raked her. 'We made a deal, Sophie Nash, but you never intended to keep your end of the bargain.' He shook her. 'Did you?' She bit her lip rather than cry out as pain shot through her scalp, filling her eyes with tears, but something must have shown on her face because he released her hair, transferring his grip to her arm before she even registered the possibility of escape. 'Did you?' he demanded.

She glared at him, her eyes huge, overbright, as she angrily refused to let the tears fall. 'Why should I? You've no right to keep me here. You've no right to destroy my work. You would have done the same in my shoes!'

'Oh, no, I wouldn't. I would never have taken the damn things in the first place,' he said savagely.

That was too much. She wrenched herself free of his grasp, flinging her fists against her hips as she launched her own attack. 'Oh, lordy!' she declared. 'You are *far* too shy, Mr Buchanan. The world must learn that hidden away in this remote corner of Malta lives one of the last of that endangered species, the *noble* male.' She raised her eyes skyward in ironic appeal. 'Heaven help me if I fall for that one.'

'Perhaps you should improve the quality of the men you. . .associate with.'

'Associate with?' she repeated in disbelief. 'Well, there's a fine, high-sounding euphemism for what you really mean.' And finally she was unable to prevent eyes brim-full of tears from overflowing, but she was too angry to care any more. She dashed her sleeve against her cheek. 'Just who do you think you are, Chay Buchanan? You lounge around here, having made enough money to retire at the advanced age of thirty——' she almost exploded '—something——'

'If you believe that, Sophie Nash, you must be mad,' he retaliated.

She was too far gone in rage to register this outburst, her pulse racketing like an express train, huge eyes sparkling darkly. 'What would you know about having to earn a living?' she charged on. 'The day-after-day grind of it? It's not all spent taking pictures in holiday islands, you know! My next booking is in Liverpool for a mail-order catalogue. Vacuum cleaners and computer games and knickers——'

She never had a chance to finish. His mouth cut off the words as it swooped to obliterate them with a kiss that owed nothing to finesse. This was no gentle caress to disarm or please her. It was the fierce stamp of authority that demanded she obey. Submit to his will. Useless to struggle, useless to fight, she knew, even as her fists pummelled at his shoulders.

Too late she sensed the subtle change, the easing of the hard grip of his hands at her waist until his long fingers were gently cradling her ribcage, the heel of his hand nudging the soft swell of her breast. By the time she realised that his mouth was no longer punishing her, was caressing her with a fierce passion that was sending her heart spiralling to the stars, it no longer mattered. Her fists had ceased their battery, had become long, slender fingers that slid up to his shoulders and clasped firmly about his neck, and her lips had parted in welcome. It was a long time before he finally raised his head to stare down at her.

'Why did you do that?' she finally whispered.

For a moment he didn't say anything. He just continued to stare at her. Then, abruptly, he turned away, ran his fingers through his dark hair, pushing it back from his forehead. 'You were getting hysterical,' he said sharply. 'I had to shut you up somehow. It was a choice between slapping you or kissing you.'

'Oh!' She took an instinctive step back, her hand flying to her mouth, as if to wipe away the taste of him. He might as well have slapped her. His words had had much the same effect. An abrupt reminder that she was in danger of making an utter fool of herself. 'Then I suppose I should be grateful.'

'Grateful?'

She lifted her shoulders slightly. 'That you chose the slightly less violent alternative. I already have enough aches and pains. Although. . .' She touched her finger to her bruised and swollen lip.

His eyes followed the gesture. 'Did I hurt you?'

'I'll recover,' she said woodenly. 'It was no worse than a slap.'

'I doubt you'd have enjoyed a slap quite so thoroughly,' he retaliated sharply.

She bit back the angry retort that flew to her tongue. He spoke no more than the truth, after all. It was time to put an end to this charade. Before she said, or did, something so unbelievably rash that she might never recover from the consequences.

The almost electric effect that Chay Buchanan had triggered from the moment she had first set eyes upon him was making her say and do things light-years away from the cool self-possession she so prided herself on. Things so wildly out of character that people she had known all her life would scarcely recognise her. Chay had seen it, had thought she was brazenly flirting to get what she wanted from him. He couldn't know that she didn't know how to flirt, that this reaction was as unwelcome to her as it was to him. But she was certain now that she had to get away before one of them exploded, because, whichever one of them it was, she was the one who would be hurt by the resulting fall-out.

If he insisted on destroying her films she could do nothing to stop him. She would find a cheap hotel, work at top speed; she knew the shots she wanted now, and that would save a considerable amount of time. There would be precious little left from her fee, but at least she would retain her reputation as a reliable photographer. And her self-control.

There were worse things in life than losing a week's

work. Far worse. She pulled herself up to the full extent of her five feet six inches. 'Do what you want with my films, Mr Buchanan,' she said. 'I want to leave here right now. I. . .I have a lot of work to catch up on.'

A small muscle was working angrily at the corner of his mouth. 'You're not going anywhere, Miss Nash. I thought I had made that quite plain.'

She made a move towards him. 'Don't you understand? You can do what you like with the wretched films. I just want to leave. Now!' she added, with some force.

'I warned you what would happen if I caught you trespassing,' he reminded her, his face hard as the cliff-face.

And the fact that he was in deadly earnest finally penetrated. 'But. . .why?'

'The reason is none of your business. But we have gone far beyond the minor problem of a few photographs. Until certain. . .negotiations have been finalised, I'm afraid I can't risk your nasty little headlines.'

'But I wouldn't——'

'You were very convincing, Sophie.'

'But. . .I didn't meant it. Truly.' She had been angry, that was all. 'I have to get home. It's——'

'What?' His lips twisted into a savage little smile. 'A matter of life and death?' His voice had an unpleasant little sneer to it that made her hackles rise, but she fought back the desire to slap him. It was too important that she convince him. 'Well?' he demanded. 'Is that what you were going to say?'

She gave an awkward little shrug. 'Perhaps I was,' she admitted, her eyes pleading with him. 'But it is. . . very important.'

'You should have thought of that before you started your sordid little job.'

She took a deep breath. 'Please let me go, Chay.' She whispered the plea, her eyes huge.

'Don't do that!' He was staring at her blankly, and for a moment she thought she was getting through to him. Then he lifted his hand to her heated cheek, to graze it with the hard edge of his thumb. 'Or I'll have to kiss you again.' His heavy-lidded eyes regarded her dispassionately. 'Until you beg me to let you stay.'

She stumbled back, but his hand was there, at her waist, to steady, hold her. 'You've got a great notion of your physical attraction,' she declared roundly, refusing to acknowledge the heat licking through her veins at the merest touch of his hand. Did that husky voice really belong to her?

'Have I?' Her eyes followed his apparent fascination with the front of her shirt, and she blushed deeply as she realised that the tips of her betraying breasts were thrusting hard against the fine cloth. His fingers traced a circle around the dark areola faintly visible against the whiteness, his thumb brushing the sensitive tip, and, apparently satisfied with her shuddering response, he raised his eyes to meet hers. 'Are you confident enough of your willpower to put it to the test?'

No! Her head screamed the word. Her mouth seemed to find it a great deal more difficult. Just as her body refused her bidding to pull away from the hand tucked against the small of her back.

What on earth was happening to her? Wild sensations were lashing at her body. Undreamed of desires that made her breasts feel tight and swollen, that heated her skin and pulsed in an almost unbearable ache deep in her loins. None of the sensations was precisely new. She was twenty-three, too old never to have felt the throb of arousal, even if she had always rejected it, afraid that because she and Jennie were twins—mirror-images of one another—it was inevitable that she must make the same mistakes.

It had been like waiting for the other shoe to drop, her mother had once told her, in a moment of weakness, on one of the few occasions she had managed to talk about it.

But she instinctively knew that what she was feeling now was different, more intense, as if the world had been nothing but a monochrome blur and had suddenly been transformed into brilliant, rainbow-bright focus.

'I. . .er. . .' She cleared her throat. 'I think I. . . perhaps. . .I. . .' There was no point in lying. He already knew.

'I think you'd better go to bed right now.'

She almost slumped against him, weak with relief that he hadn't actually put her to the test. Then, panicking that he would misread the signals her body was flashing out like a firebug in heat, she tried to yank free of his drugging touch. 'No! That is. . . I didn't mean. . .'

'Didn't you, Sophie?' He shrugged slightly. 'Shame your body wasn't co-operating.' But before she could protest he had stepped back. 'I'll show you to your room.' He paused briefly as they passed the table, and gathered up her camera bag. 'And, in case you're wondering, this will be locked away with the rest of your belongings, where you can't get at it. So don't get any bright ideas about running off in the middle of the night.'

A yawn caught her unawares, as if to demonstrate that she wasn't capable of running anywhere. She was suddenly quite exhausted, and it took all her strength simply not to lean against him. 'I couldn't run on the spot,' she murmured.

'You'll forgive my natural scepticism. It's stood me in good stead so far.'

His words were like a douche of cold water, driving all thought of sleep from her head. 'You are unbearable!' she exclaimed.

'You'll find that "unbearable" is one of my more endearing characteristics.' His fierce glance choked off the rejoinder that sprang to her lips. 'Upstairs, Sophie. Now.'

The sun woke her, dragging her reluctantly from sleep. But the brightness was not to be resisted, and Sophie opened gritty lids to acknowledge the day. The light was streaming in clear and bright through the open window and she stretched, tentatively trying out her aching limbs. She was stiff, it was true, but only her shoulder still gave her any real pain, and that was something she could live with. It was certainly no more unbearable than Chay Buchanan.

She sat up, eased her feet to the cool polished boards and went across to the window. Her room was on the opposite side of the tower from Chay's bedroom and the terrace, overlooking a flat stretch of open ground before the land began to rise beyond the road in the rocky terraces of small farms.

The week before she had cursed the squall of spring rain that had delayed her work. But now tiny irises, no bigger than her thumb, bee orchids and other small flowers were spreading a thick carpet of bloom across the baked earth, and a hedge of mimosa was decked out in fluffy yellow blooms.

Reluctantly she turned from the window. No time for that. The sooner she was ready, the sooner she could leave, and get on with the business of explaining to puzzled hoteliers why she had to repeat her work.

She went into the bathroom that adjoined her bedroom and stood for a few moments until the needlesharp spray of the shower had her gasping. Then she

washed her hair, threatening herself for the hundredth
time that she would have the tiresome mop cut as she
combed it out and dried it with the battery-operated
drier that went everywhere with her. Her hair kinked
at the slightest hint of humidity, despite every atttempt
to tame it. It was only the fear that if she had it cut it
would make her look like a poodle that had so far kept
the scissors at bay. At least long she could clamp it
down with hairpins, if all else failed.

Theresa had unpacked her clothes and laid out her
cosmetics on the dressing-table, as if Sophie were a
lady. But she had no time to waste on make-up. She
quickly tugged on a fresh chambray shirt and long
tailored navy shorts that echoed the pair she had
'borrowed' from Chay the night before.

She pushed her feet into a pair of sandals and
buckled on the watch that had appeared beside her bed
since she fell into an almost immediate and dreamless
sleep the night before. Had he put it there while she
slept? She shrugged away the thought. It hardly mattered. But, as she pulled the strap tight, her fingers
shook a little at the thought of him standing over her
defenceless sleeping body.

Stop it, she warned herself. He might have kissed
her, but it wasn't because he desired her. He'd made
that more than plain. She glanced in the mirror and
after a moment fastened one more button of her shirt,
leaving only the top button open. She didn't want a
repetition of his accusation that she was batting eyelashes or anything else at him. It was too important
that she convince him to let her go. He *had* to let her
go. She opened the wardrobe door, took an armful of
clothes and flung them on to the bed ready to pack.
But there was no suitcase.

She took a deep breath, opened the bedroom door
and marched downstairs, determined to thrash it out

with him. But Chay wasn't there, only Theresa, greeting her as an old friend, drawing her excitedly into the kitchen and sitting her down at the table. It was difficult to follow what the woman was saying—she switched from Maltese to English and back again without apparently noticing. But, as she produced coffee, melting scrambled eggs and bacon, it gradually became clear that she was expressing her delight that Miss Sophie was going to look after Tom while she was away.

Sophie opened her mouth to protest that this was just not possible. But Theresa, beaming, removed her apron and donned an impressive black hat. '*Grazzi*, Miss Sophie, *grazzi, hafna,*' she repeated, taking her hand in both of hers and shaking it vigorously, departing once more into her own language.

'Theresa,' she interrupted urgently.

'*Iva*?'

'Where is Mr Buchanan?'

'He's out. At his marina.' Marina? At a time like this, he had decided to go boating? Sophie was stunned by the sheer nerve of the man, but it didn't matter where he was. She had a chance to escape. But Theresa hadn't finished. 'Tom. . .he is in the garden.'

She pulled Sophie to the door. Tom looked up from the small enclosed garden below the terrace, that was sheltered from the cool April breeze blowing in from the Mediterranean. He was playing with a large yellow toy crane, shifting a pile of sand to an equally handsome dumper-truck. The child was an unlikely gaoler, Sophie thought. But just as effective as chains.

'Hello, Tom.'

'Hello,' he said, suddenly shy.

'I go now,' Theresa declared, and turned to leave.

'No, wait!' The woman paused, eyebrows slightly raised at the touch of panic in her voice. 'When will Mr Buchanan be back?' Sophie continued, more carefully.

Theresa shrugged. 'Later.'

Later. That was just great. But she might usefully take advantage of his absence to regain control of her possessions so that she could make a run for it when he did get back. 'Do you know what he has done with my camera? My car keys?'

'No worry.' The woman patted Sophie's hand. 'Safe.' She indicated the rapidly cooling breakfast. 'Eat!'

'And my suitcase?' she persisted. At least she could pack in readiness for his return.

'Upstairs.' Theresa pointed at the ceiling.

Sophie sank into the chair. It wasn't much help, but it was a start. 'Thank you, Theresa,' she said, temporarily resigned to her fate. At least until the return of Mr Chay Buchanan. 'Have a good holiday.'

CHAPTER FIVE

SOPHIE stared at her breakfast, furious and yet oddly touched that Chay had trusted her sufficiently to leave Tom in her care. She glanced at the dark-haired boy visible through the open door. How could he have been so sure she wouldn't just walk out and leave him? After all, if she was everything he believed. . .

Idiot! Who did she think she was kidding? Of course she was going to stay. He had her camera locked away as assurance for her good behaviour. And her passport. Even her suitcase. Sophie Nash wasn't going anywhere until Chay Buchanan was good and ready.

She glared at her breakfast. She would go on hunger strike. He would have to let her go then. She stood up and seized the plate, determined to smash it and its contents against the nearest wall. One thing stopped her. The absolute certainty that he would derive great pleasure from making her clear up the mess. She sank back into her chair. Besides, she was hungry.

She washed her dish and placed it on the rack and glanced around. If she was going to cook the child lunch, she'd better know what was available.

She swung open the huge fridge door, checking over the contents. Then she stopped. What on earth was she doing? She would be getting out the vacuum cleaner next, to run over the living-room carpet. Coming to heel like a well-trained dog. She slammed the fridge door shut and turned to find herself being regarded solemnly by a pair of almost black eyes. Not that mysterious ocean-green like his father's.

'Is it time for lunch, Miss Nash?' Tom asked tentatively.

'Lunch?' She glanced at her watch. Half-past ten. Ten! Could she really have slept that late? She looked at her watch again. Apparently she could. Tom was watching her anxiously and she smiled reassuringly, saving her anger for his father, and crouched down so that she was on his level. 'Not yet, Tom. Perhaps elevenses. What would you like?' she asked.

'Honey?' he suggested hopefully.

'Bread and honey?' He nodded. 'Milk?'

'Yes, please,' he said, and wriggled on to a kitchen chair. 'Miss Nash?'

'Why don't you call me Sophie?' she suggested, reaching for a crusty loaf of homemade bread. Homemade? If Mr Chay Buchanan expected her to pound dough on his behalf he had another think coming. She had never made bread in her life.

Tom looked doubtful. 'Papa said I was to call you Miss Nash.'

'Did he? What else did he say?'

'I must be polite and. . .and not make you cross, or you won't stay and look after me while Theresa's away.'

Well, clever old Papa. What a pity he didn't take his own advice. 'I'd like you to call me Sophie, Tom. Then we can be friends.'

He immediately brightened. 'OK. Sophie. Will you swim with me this afternoon?'

She looked at the boy's hopeful face, but wouldn't make a promise she might not be able to keep. 'I might not be here,' she said.

'Papa said you were staying until Theresa comes back.'

'Did he?' Well, Papa could think again. 'You're a very good swimmer,' she said.

'How do you know that?'

She handed the boy a thick slice of bread spread with honey. 'I saw you yesterday——' And then she stopped. She didn't want to think about the cliff. 'What would you like for lunch, Tom?' she asked quickly, to divert his thoughts. To divert her own thoughts.

'Honey?' he sugested.

'I don't think so.' They settled on pizza, then Tom took her outside to show her the garden.

Dr Manduca found them there, sitting in the fragrant shade of a carob tree thick with pink blossom. 'You look better today, Miss Nash. No, please don't get up.'

'I feel fine,' she replied.

'Good. I saw Chay in Valletta this morning. He said you were brighter. He's left you babysitting, I understand?'

'I'm not a baby,' Tom said. 'I'm nearly six.'

The doctor laughed. '*Very* nearly six,' he agreed. 'On Sunday, in fact.'

'How do you know?'

'Because I was there when you were born. Are you having a party?' The boy shrugged and the doctor's eyes softened. 'I'll have to remind your Papa. My children will be very disappointed if you don't.'

Tom turned to Sophie. 'Would you come to my party, Sophie?'

'I. . .don't know if I'll be here, Tom.'

'But Theresa's going to be away for a whole week,' he replied with a small frown.

'Run along and play with your truck, Tom,' the doctor said, unexpectedly coming to her rescue. 'I just want to look at Miss Nash.'

'I'm fine, really,' Sophie protested.

'Shall I be the judge of that?' But when he had checked her over he agreed. 'Just as well, since you're looking after Tom.' He smiled as he closed his bag.

'It's good of you to offer to cover for Theresa. She rarely gets a break. Not that she complains. Bring him over to play with my brood one day,' he suggested. 'I'll get Gian to arrange something.' He stood up. 'Have a good holiday. And no more climbing, eh?'

She offered what sounded horribly like a hollow echo to his cheerful laughter. 'No,' she promised. 'I plan to steer well clear of the cliff from now on.' She walked with him to the door, shook his hand and watched as his car pulled away. She must be mad, she thought. If she had just told the doctor the whole story, he would almost certainly have talked some sense into Chay. She closed the door and leaned against it. All supposing Dr Manduca would believe her. The men were friends and men stuck together. No. She had got herself into this stupid situation and she would have to get herself out of it.

After lunch Tom went upstairs for a nap. He seemed a little old for this, but Sophie had noticed that children stayed up much later here than at home. They all seemed to sleep in the afternoon. And it suited her very well. With Chay out and Tom asleep, it was as good a chance as she was likely to get to search for her things.

She began upstairs. Theresa had said the suitcase was up there and that was a start. But a quick tour of Chay's room proved fruitless. The only hiding place large enough was the wardrobe, but that revealed nothing beyond a well-tended selection of clothes. She had begun to close the door when she noticed a small card on the floor. A business card. It must have dropped out of a pocket. She bent and picked it up. The logo, a dark green tower, belonged to Castile Developments. She had seen it all over the islands on construction sites and at the new marina, even at a hotel she had photographed that had had the developer's board still in place. It was one of the biggest companies on the island. But what on earth. . .? A stirring from Tom's room sent a warning prickle across her scalp.

She slipped the card into her pocket and hurried on to the landing, but when she peeked into the child's room he had simply rolled over and was still fast asleep. But it was a warning that she didn't have time to waste on speculation.

There was a flight of stairs leading to the next floor and she took it, expecting to find a similar layout to the first floor. But the stairs ended in a small landing, with further progress blocked by a heavy door. She seized the handle and pushed. Nothing happened, and she didn't need much convincing that throwing herself at it would damage her far more than the door.

On a hunch, she stretched on her toes and felt along the small ledge above the frame. Nothing. Disappointed, she gave the door a sharp kick to relieve her feelings. She glanced at her watch. Tom wouldn't sleep for much longer, and the knowledge that Chay might return at any moment lent further urgency to her search.

The study was the most likely hiding place for her camera bag and she could always throw her clothes in the back of the car. If she could find the keys.

Impatiently she tugged at the desk drawer, expecting it, too, to be locked. It slid smoothly open to reveal a stack of lined writing-blocks close-covered with a bold masculine script. A tiny flicker of excitement raised her pulse-rate and just a few lines confirmed her suspicion that she had stumbled across the first Chay Buchanan novel for six years. Was this his big secret? For a moment her fingers hovered over the smooth paper. . .

Then she snatched her hand back and closed the drawer quickly. No time for that.

The long centre drawer contained nothing more exciting than pens and pencils and other small writing accessories.

The last drawer contained notepaper and envelopes. On an impulse she wrote a brief note to the neighbour who looked after her flat while she was away, warning her that it might be for a few more days. She would ask Chay to post it for her. He could only say no. On reflection, he would almost certainly say no. But maybe she would get the chance to post it herself. She returned to the centre drawer, pulling it wider in her search for stamps. No stamps, but something else. A key. To the upstairs room? Her fingers began to close on it, then she saw something else.

A small photograph in a frame. It was a girl. A girl whose eyes glowed with happiness. She was dark and beautiful. In the corner she had written, 'Forever, Maria'. Sophie had thought that Tom looked like his father. But he had his mother's beautiful dark eyes.

The click of the door-latch was like a bullet, shattering her reverie. With a guilty start she hurriedly pushed the photograph back where she had found it and closed the drawer, leaping to her feet, her heart hammering, an excuse forming on her lips. But when she turned round it was not the accusing eyes of Chay Buchanan that confronted her.

'Well, sweetheart, this is cosy.' And Nigel Phillips sauntered into the study.

'Nigel? Where on earth have you sprung from?' Confusion, relief, made her shrill.

'That's not a very warm welcome for a friend who's come all the way from London to look you up,' he said.

Sophie knew she should be glad to see him. He

represented an immediate source of rescue. But she was far more concerned with Chay's reaction should he return and find them together in his study. 'H-how did you get in?'

'The front door wasn't locked,' he said, moving over to the desk and eyeing the computer. 'Country folk are so trusting.'

He reached for the switch and she grabbed his hand. 'Don't touch!' His pale blue eyes regarded her strangely. 'He'll know if you turn it on,' she said. 'The timer. . .'

'And he'll know you've been snooping.' He grinned. 'What a bright girl you are, Sophie. We'll make a good team. What have you found out so far?'

She jerked her hand back, sickened at the implication. 'You must go. . .he'll be back in a minute.'

'Don't panic. I've no intention of interrupting your little idyll, my sweet. It's just that when you didn't turn up with your photographs, I thought you might be planning to renege on our little deal.'

'No——'

'You weren't at your flat,' he continued, turning his attention to the drawers, 'and when I phoned your hotel they told me you'd booked out two days ago. So I thought I'd better find out what was happening.'

'I'll tell you what's happening,' she said. 'He caught me taking photographs with a long lens and he's keeping me here. . . He won't let me go, Nigel.'

'Really? I can't see any chains,' Nigel replied, with a knowing little smile. 'But then, men like him don't need them.'

'What is that supposed to mean?' she demanded, but a searing blush betrayed her.

'Come on, sweetheart, there's no need to be bashful. I'm really pleased with you.' He lightly flicked her cheek. 'Really pleased. I didn't think you had it in you.'

She stepped back sharply, hating him to touch her. 'What. . .? What do you mean?'

He grinned. 'You'll be able to give me a whole lot more than a photograph now, won't you?'

'I. . .I don't understand.' But there could be no mistaking his meaning, and he drove the message home without mercy.

'If you want to find your sister,' he said, with a leer that turned her blood cold.

'For pity's sake, Nigel. . .'

'I'll give you a few days.'

'But. . . You expect me to stay here?'

'You'll stay,' he said confidently. 'Not for me. For Jennie.' He stroked his hand down her cheek in a gesture that made her skin crawl, and she jerked away. 'Relax, sweetheart. Anyone would think. . .' He shrugged. 'There's no need to feel guilty about enjoying yourself. It's for your sister, right? I'll park up the road after dark. . .when? Sunday? Will that give you enough time? I'll flash my headlights at about ten o'clock. Just make sure you have all the juicy details. There'll be a nice little bonus in it for you.'

'I don't want a bonus. Or your filthy money.'

'That's up to you.' He shrugged. 'But your sister might be glad of it. The last time I saw her——' He shook his head. 'Some of those bed and breakfast places. . .'

Pain stabbed at her. She had been kidding herself for long enough. 'All right! I get the picture.' All pretence of a 'little favour' was at an end. This was blackmail. His hand reached for the drawer with the photograph. Sophie swallowed. How far back had she pushed it? 'You'd better go before Chay gets back,' she said urgently, but Nigel had already straightened and was staring at the doorway. Sophie's head swam as the blood drained from her face, and she held her breath, waiting for the explosion.

'Hello, there. What's your name?'

'I'm Tom.' As she heard the childish voice she almost sobbed with relief. 'Who are you?'

'I'm Nigel. I'm a friend of Sophie's.'

'Nigel's just leaving, Tom. Why don't you go and get into your swimming costume?' Tom needed no second bidding, and, giving Nigel a little smile, he disappeared.

'Who's the kid?'

'The housekeeper's boy.' He stared at her, taking in the bright colour that stained the pallor of her cheeks. She had always been incapable of telling a lie. 'She's away for a couple of days.' She walked quickly to the front door. 'You'd better go, Nigel,' she said.

'What's the hurry? I'd like a look around while you're on your own.' He moved towards the living-room door.

'I'm expecting Chay back any minute.' He hesitated, suspicious of her anxiety to be rid of him. 'He's late already,' she said, straightening, her voice a little firmer. 'Unless, of course, you would like to stay and meet him?' she invited. 'I have a feeling he would enjoy the opportunity of a word with you.'

'I take your point.'

She was shaking when she closed the door, locking it after him and leaning weakly back against it. She hadn't realised until this morning just how truly despicable the man was. He knew where her sister was, but his price for the information had been a photograph of Chay Buchanan in his hideaway. In her desperation it had seemed small enough. But it wasn't small, she discovered. She felt as if she had been touched by something very nasty, and she shuddered.

'I'm ready now, Sophie.' Tom's voice seemed to come from miles away. 'Sophie?' He tugged at her hand.

She glanced towards the study, the key, the possibility of freedom. It would have to wait.

A few minutes later, Sophie stood on the edge of the pool. She had no illusions about the water. It was too early in the year for it to be warm. But she welcomed that. It would be cold and clean and would wash away the touch of Nigel Phillips. Tom dived in without hesitation. She would have liked to follow his example, but her shoulder was in no condition for such a jolt and she lowered herself in, catching her breath as the water reached her stomach.

It was not water to hang around in, and she began to swim up and down the pool at a brisk pace. She was beginning to flag when a splash startled her. She had been so determined to keep a close watch on Tom that she had not seen Chay until his head surfaced beside her.

'Enjoying yourself?' he asked, with the kind of smile that suggested he knew exactly what she was suffering and was enjoying every moment of it.

'It's very. . .bracing.'

He laughed, disconcertingly, displaying a set of even white teeth. 'You should try it in winter.'

'No, thanks. In fact, since you're here now, I think I'll get out before I succumb to hypothermia.'

'Nonsense. It's not cold.' A pair of strong hands caught her around the waist and pulled her down. She came up, spluttering and gasping for air.

'You——' She didn't get a chance to call him the name that sprang to her lips because he ducked her again. The second time she erupted, gasping, from the water, she didn't bother with insults. She needed all her breath for retaliation.

The immediacy of her response, the shock of her hands crashing into his shoulders as she launched herself at him, took Chay by surprise. But he recovered instantly, and as he was knocked backwards by her furious onslaught his arms snaked around her waist, and he pulled her down with him, twisting over in the water so that he was above her and in control. And he was right. As his legs tangled against hers, and his arm pinioned her against his broad chest and hard flat stomach, she was no longer cold.

As he surfaced with her he grinned broadly. 'Better?' he asked.

Immeasurably better. Stupidly, dangerously better. Her hands were clinging to his shoulders, his skin was smooth beneath her fingers and the water pinned her against him. How much better could it get?

At that moment Tom leapt on them and Chay released her, turning with a roar to dunk the boy, chasing him up the pool in mock rage. Then they both turned on Sophie. With a little scream she struck out for the side of the pool. Chay's hand caught her ankle just as she reached the safety of the edge of the pool and he hauled her back. She twisted in the water, determined to fend him off, but he caught her round the waist, holding her up, so that despite her furious kicks she was quite helpless. For a moment something sparked in the depths of his eyes as they roved her body, and she caught her breath. But when he tightened his grasp around her waist it was simply to lift her up and sit her on the side of the pool.

'You are free to go, ma'am,' he said, with measured irony, and then quite deliberately removed his hands. 'For now.' It was oddly disturbing. As if he had been reinforcing his ability to hold her for as long as he wished.

Sophie scrambled to her feet and stepped back out

of his reach. Turning away to pick up a towel that she had dropped on a nearby rock, she began drying her hair with furious concentration. But she could not resist Tom's yells of delight as his father threw him up in the air, Chay's shouts of feigned rage as the boy's splashes found their mark.

She sank on to the rock, watching the two of them. The graceful little minnow swimming beside the shark. Tom a small promise of the man beside him. Chay, his body rippling with contained power, holding back as he swam alongside his son. Sophie scarcely realised that she was smiling. Then Chay rolled on to his back, and as their eyes met he smiled too. The smile of one adult to another in their conspiracy to amuse a child.

She immediately became absorbed in the meticulous drying of the ends of her hair, and when she looked again he had turned away to scoop up Tom and dump him on the side of the pool before hauling himself out.

She wrapped Tom in a towel and began to rub him dry. 'I'll see to Tom,' Chay said, taking over from her. She almost jumped as his shoulder brushed her arm, feeling suddenly very naked as his eyes flickered over her modest fuchsia one-piece bathing suit. He glanced up. 'You'd better go and make some tea,' he said, dismissing her. 'Plenty of milk for Tom.'

Her eyes snapped. 'Is that what Theresa would do?'

'She wouldn't have to be told.'

She opened her mouth, firmly resolved to tell him to go and make his own tea. But confronted with his broad tanned body, clad only in a scrap of black material that accentuated rather than concealed his blatant masculinity, and the spread of dark hair that curled across his chest, down his flat belly to his loins, she simply swallowed. 'Right,' she said, backing away, then she turned and fled.

Her hand shook as she filled the kettle. 'This is

ridiculous,' she said out loud to herself. 'Get a grip of yourself, girl. He's just a man.' An arrogant bully of a man, who had made his feelings on the subject of Miss Sophie Nash very clear. And, while the kettle was boiling, Miss Sophie Nash would be well advised to go and cover herself up. She had made the hallway when the front doorbell rang.

Sophie physically jumped. Had Nigel changed his mind? Come back for her? The peremptory ring was repeated rather more vigorously, and she moved quickly to open it before Chay heard and came to investigate.

It was difficult to say who was more startled—the elegant woman on the doorstep, who looked as if she had stepped out of the pages of a glossy magazine, possibly in her late thirties, although it would take a practised eye to tell for certain, dressed by Jean Muir in a pastel suit that was neither blue nor grey but the most sophisticated merging of the two, and with sleek dark hair fresh from the stylist, or Sophie, in her damply clinging swimsuit and with salt-stiffened hair drying out into what her mother unkindly described as something resembling tow.

The other woman regained her voice first. 'Poppy Curzon,' she said coolly. 'Please tell Chay that I'm here.' And she stepped over the threshold without invitation.

Sophie stiffened at the woman's tone. She had spoken to her as if she was a servant. And if she was going to be treated like one, she was quite capable of acting the part. 'Is he expecting you, Miss Curzon?' she asked, in her best starched imitation of a maid.

But the question was academic. She brushed past Sophie, her face wreathed in smiles, her arms extended theatrically. 'Chay, darling.'

'Chay, darling' had taken the trouble to pull on a

polo shirt and a pair of shorts over his swimsuit and suddenly Sophie felt very underdressed.

'Poppy.' Chay took the newcomer in his arms and kissed her warmly on the cheek. 'Why didn't you let me know you were coming? I would have come to the airport.'

'Join the twentieth century and install a telephone and I will, darling.'

'Not a hope,' he laughed, obviously delighted to see the woman. 'Come on through to the garden. We're just having tea. Bring an extra cup, Sophie.'

At this reference to Sophie, Poppy turned, and gave her the kind of speculative glance that despite its fleeting nature would have earned a man a slap. 'Have you finally replaced Theresa with a younger model, darling?' she asked, with a small suggestive laugh. 'I do hope she can cook as well.'

For a moment Sophie's grey eyes flashed thunder and lightning, but Chay intervened before she could say anything outrageous.

'Poppy, meet Miss Sophie Nash,' he said, introducing her with grave formality. 'She's Tom's nanny.' His look was a sharp warning.

'Isn't he a little old for a nanny?'

'It's a temporary arrangement.'

Sophie drew in a sharp breath at this brazen lie.

But this time Poppy forestalled the threatened explosion. 'Very temporary, I should imagine, by the look of those goose-pimples. If she doesn't get dressed soon she's going to catch her death of cold.'

'Darling, if you wanted a nanny you should have let me know. I would have found someone for you. Someone properly trained.'

Sophie arrived just in time to hear Poppy's remark, to witness the long white fingers with immaculately polished nails curved possessively around Chay's arm. She placed the tray of tea very carefully on the garden table, catching sight of her own battered nails and hands and wincing at the comparison.

'She is trained, Poppy,' Chay said evenly, insolent eyes meeting Sophie's without the slightest shame. She had taken a quick shower and dressed, but with her hair still damp she was conscious of looking rather less like an old English nanny in the Norland tradition than an old English sheepdog. No competition for the well-groomed elegance of Poppy Curzon.

Poppy evidently agreed. Having turned a searching eye upon her, she finally asked, 'In what?'

'I promise you,' Chay said, with a very thin smile, 'she's utterly dedicated to her job. You've only brought two cups, Sophie. Go and fetch another.'

'I have to organise Tom's tea,' she said quickly. She had no wish to be a part of his cosy tête-à-tête with Poppy Curzon. And it was more than plain from the fixed smile on the other woman's face that she harboured no lingering desire for Sophie's company either.

But Chay had other ideas. 'Tom's gone down to the stables with Twany,' he said. 'He won't be back for at least an hour and, as you can see, Poppy can't wait to grill you on your qualifications.'

Twany? Who was Twany? But Sophie met his glance. If she was to be cast in the role of nanny, the least she could do was make some pretence of doing her job. She pursed her lips, in a manner perfected by her grandmother. 'I do hope,' she said primly, 'that you dried Tom thoroughly before he went.'

'Have you forgotten so soon?' he asked, his voice a silken ambush. 'How very thorough I can be?' The colour flooded to her cheeks at this reference to the way he had showered her. And dried her. Her stupid mouth should be fitted with a zip-fastener.

'I'll fetch that cup.' Anything to get away from his sardonic eyes and the flicker of amusement that crossed the lips of Poppy Curzon. Amusement that clearly suggested she was wasting her time if she thought Chay Buchanan would ever take more than a passing interest in the likes of her.

I don't want him to take an interest in me, she swore silently, as she clung to the edge of the kitchen table and tried to ignore the soft ripple of laughter that floated through the kitchen door, tried to fight down an almost irresistible urge to throw something. I just want to get away from here. Away from Chay Buchanan.

She was still simmering as she passed around Theresa's excellent cake. 'Are you here on holiday, Miss Curzon?' she asked, with excessive politeness.

'Holiday?' The idea clearly took the woman by surprise. 'No, I'm here on business.' She shrugged. 'I am Chay's literary agent.'

'Was, darling,' he corrected her. 'Since I no longer write, I don't need an agent.'

'Of course you do. It may be a while since your last novel, but I'm still handling overseas sales, reprints, translations. There's a repeat of the mini-series of your first book scheduled for this autumn.' Chay did not look paticularly pleased with this news. 'There's an enormous amount of interest still, darling. You could name your own price.'

'I don't understand,' Sophie said, and they both turned to her.

'What don't you understand?' Poppy snapped, clearly wishing that the 'nanny' would remember her place.

Sophie kept her eyes fixed upon the tall, glowering figure of her nemesis. 'I don't understand why Chay said he doesn't write any more.' Poppy's eyes narrowed, but Sophie was transfixed by the momentary flash of disbelief that crossed Chay's face. 'He writes every day of his life. He told me so himself.' Take that, Mr Buchanan, her eyes clearly told him. You might be able to keep me your prisoner and amuse your sophisticated women-friends at my expense, but you can't gag me. Then, as his eyes turned to steel, she suddenly wasn't so sure.

But before the explosion happened, before he could say or do anything, Poppy exclaimed, 'A new book? Tell me? What are you working on, Chay?'

From across the table his eyes finally relinquished their hold on Sophie, but she was left in no doubt that retaliation had only been delayed. And when he turned slowly to Poppy, he was wearing a small, disparaging smile. It was a daunting display of self-control. 'I'm afraid that Sophie is mistaken.'

Poppy glanced at Sophie. 'But she said——'

'That I write every day?' He shrugged. 'I keep a diary. Doesn't everyone?'

For a moment she was speechless. 'But Chay, that would be——'

'It's not for publication,' he said sharply. Then, as he saw from Poppy's intent expression that he had only aroused her interest further, he leaned back in his chair. 'I hardly think two hundred and fifty pages of "Got up. *Lounged* around——"' he looked pointedly at Sophie as he repeated the word she had used in her withering description of his lifestyle '"—went to bed" is likely to hit the bestseller list, Poppy.'

Poppy stared at him, then at Sophie, picking up the dangerous undercurrent that tugged between them. 'That would depend on who you went to bed with, darling,' she murmured, and a secret little smile curved her lips as she met Sophie's eyes.

'Kiss and tell was never my style, Poppy,' he said. 'In fact, I'm far too busy these days to——'

'I know. I've seen Castile Developments everywhere, sweetheart, and I'm very impressed, but that's not you. . .'

'It is now.'

Sophie's brows flew up in surprise. 'Castile Developments?' Her fingers touched the card in her pocket. 'Is that you?'

'Didn't you know?' Poppy asked, apparently amused.

But Sophie, staring at Chay, didn't bother to answer. It was hardly surprising he had taken umbrage at her assertion that he had 'retired'. The only surprise was that he had time to put pen to paper at all. But there *was* a book. But since he clearly had no intention of publishing it, there was something else driving him to keep her prisoner.

But Poppy hadn't given up. 'You could leave the management of the development company to someone else, Chay. Anybody could do that. But you have a gift.' His gesture was dismissive. 'Well, think of Tom,' she pressed him. 'You have his future to consider. For a three-book contract we would be talking telephone numbers.'

'Perhaps. But this way I don't have to stand up and bare my soul every time I complete a deal. Writing was something I did a long time ago. I don't do it any more because the books are not enough. They want more and more—chat-shows, interviews, lecture-tours—and when they have all that, and they can't think of anything pleasant to say, it gets more personal. . .' His glance at Sophie was quelling. 'They never give up.'

'Chay, I promise——'

He stopped her with a look. 'Don't promise what you can't deliver, Poppy. Somewhere in that contract, in words so obscure, so small that it'll need a magnifying glass to find them there will be a water-tight clause about the author co-operating with publicity. There always is,' he said bitterly, 'as I know to my cost.'

'The absolute minimum, I promise.'

Sophie almost winced as he turned hard, provoking eyes upon her. 'You see, Sophie, that I was able to sharpen my natural scepticism on an expert.' But she rose to the challenge.

'You never seemed to object to co-operating with publicity in the past,' she retaliated. 'You always appeared to be extremely happy in the photographs that were printed in the newspapers.'

'And the camera never lies?' His eyes were expressionless. He replaced his cup on the table. 'I'm sorry you've had a pointless journey, Poppy.'

'Not pointless,' Poppy said, and once more her hand strayed to his arm. 'Come and have dinner with me tonight, Chay.' Her voice was husky. 'It'll be like old times.'

'Excuse me.' Sophie stood up abruptly, and swept the tray back to the kitchen.

When Chay had seen Poppy to her taxi he leaned against the kitchen table, watching while Sophie concentrated very hard on washing the dishes. She made it last a long time, knowing full well that he was waiting for her to turn and face the music. Finally, however, it was done, and the moment could be put off no longer. She stripped off the over-large rubber gloves she had found in the cupboard beneath the sink and took a deep breath to calm the butterflies dancing in her stomach.

'So, you won't be in for dinner tonight?' she asked brightly as she turned to face him.

'No, unfortunately, because you must be quite a

cook. If that demonstration of stirring is anything to go
by.'

'If you think that's all there is to cooking, you have
clearly never tried it yourself.'

'Never,' he confirmed, folding his arms. There was
something about the way he said it that made her doubt
the truth of that statement.

'Who is Twany?' she asked, abruptly changing the
subject.

'He's Theresa's brother. He looks after the horses
and does the gardening.'

'Then I'm surprised you haven't given him the week
off as well. However did you resist the temptation to
set me weeding and mucking out the stables?'

He took a step towards her, and she almost flinched
as she saw the warning glint in his eyes, edging back
until the sink brought her to a halt. 'It was tough,
Sophie Nash, I promise.' He caught hold of her hands,
held up as if to ward him off, and turned them over to
look at her palms. 'But unfortunately these are in no
state to wield a shovel.'

She ignored with difficulty the ripple of excitement
at his touch as he cradled her hands. The memory of
Poppy Curzon's throaty voice helped. 'What a great
disappointment that must be for you!'

He stared at her fingers, still bearing the marks of
her desperate scramble up the cliff. When he looked
up all trace of gentleness had disappeared. 'Perhaps
they'll be sufficiently healed for you to put in a day or
two before you leave.'

'Why don't you go the whole way and put me to
work on one of your construction sites?'

'Don't tempt me!'

'Forget it, Chay,' she said. 'I'm leaving today. Right
now, in fact!'

His grip tightened painfully on her fingers. 'No,

Sophie. You'll stay for as long as I choose to keep you here.'

'You can't!' He didn't answer. He didn't need to. 'How long?' she asked, a little shakily.

'A week. Maybe a little more. So take a few days' holiday and forget why you came here. I do mean that.'

'This is your idea of a holiday?' she demanded.

'Tom's not hard work.'

'I've no objection to Tom's company,' she retorted pointedly.

'Then looking after him for a few days will be precious little penance for all the trouble you've put me to.' Sophie took a breath, but he hadn't finished. 'I sent away your films this morning.'

'Oh!' The exclamation escaped in a little rush of air. Despite her attempt to deceive him he had still kept to his part of the bargain. 'Where?' she asked anxiously. 'Which laboratory did you send them to?'

'You don't really expect me to tell you that?' he demanded, and she gave a little gasp. Always, she forgot. The minute he touched her she forgot everything. She snatched her hands away and he smiled slightly. 'You needn't worry. I took advice. They'll be of professional quality,' he promised.

'Thank you,' she said stiffly.

His eyebrows rose dramatically. 'Can this be gratitude?' he enquired.

She ignored the sarcasm. 'How long will they be?'

'Why? Do you have something more important to do? Some other unsuspecting soul to point your long lens at?'

'No, I don't!' Once had been enough. More than enough.

'Then, what's your hurry?' He shrugged. 'Theresa

wanted to go and see her latest grandchild. She should be back in about a week.'

'But you're not keeping me here to give Theresa a holiday, are you, Chay?' she demanded. 'You just want her out of the way, because if she knew you were keeping me here against my will she wouldn't stand for it. Would she? So what's the real reason?'

CHAPTER SIX

Chay glared at her. 'That is none of your damn business, Sophie Nash. All you have to do is behave yourself for a few days, then you can go.'

'How many days?' she demanded.

'As many as it takes!' For a moment the air crackled as the two of them squared up to each other. Then he swept a hand through the lock of hair that had fallen across his brow. 'Believe me when I tell you that I don't want you hanging around any longer than necessary. I spent today trying to move. . .certain matters forward.'

What 'certain matters'? She made a determined effort to dampen her natural curiosity. She didn't want to know. She didn't want to know anything. But she regarded him with disapproval. 'You took a heck of a chance leaving Tom alone with me. Suppose I had just walked out and left him?' A worse thought struck her. 'Suppose something had happened to him? There's no telephone, no car——'

'I gave up leaving anything to chance years ago,' he said abruptly. 'Twany was near by, keeping an eye on things.'

'And to stop me leaving?' she demanded.

'Leaving? And where would you have gone, pray? On foot, without any money or a passport? I don't think so. But the true reason for your stay remains our secret.'

'Your secret,' she amended. 'One of them.'

'The only one you'll be privy to.'

'How many do you have?' She squared up to him

again. 'For instance, is it common knowledge that you own Castile Develoments?'

His hand shot out and grasped her arm. 'It's what I do here.' Not all he did, she thought. But she had already said far too much. She didn't want him to know she had been prying through his desk. He released her. 'I'm a businessman. A very good one. There's no scandal in that.'

'None,' she agreed quickly.

'So. We'll keep the reason for your stay between the two of us. Clearly you prefer it that way, or you would have spilled the beans to Poppy.'

'You saw to it that I didn't have much opportunity for that. Was that why you insisted I stay for the tea ceremony? To keep me from writing a cry for help and slipping it into her car?'

'How bright you are, Sophie,' he said quietly. 'What a pity to waste all that beauty and intelligence on such a sordid occupation.' He regarded her thoughtfully. 'You're right, of course. And if you could have alerted Poppy you would have had an ally.'

'Would I?' She gave an awkward little shrug. 'It didn't feel much like it.'

'Didn't it?' He laughed softly. 'Then you were wrong. If Poppy had known your true purpose in being here she would have fallen upon you like a long-lost sister.'

'A long lost——?' She stopped. Took a deep breath. It was just a figure of speech. He knew nothing about the real reason why it had been so important to get a photograph of him.

But he was frowning. 'What is it? What did I say?'

'Nothing. It was nothing.' Change the subject. Something. Anything. 'I. . .I think it's a pity you don't publish what you write,' she said quickly. To her relief she saw that Chay was amused.

'That came perilously close to a compliment.'

'You don't need me to tell you how good you are. Were,' she corrected herself carefully. 'I. . .I have some sympathy with Poppy. It must be infuriating to have represented one of the hottest literary properties in the world, only to have him. . .drop out.'

'She has other authors,' he replied, the smile switched off as quickly as it had appeared.

That was better. It was easier when he was angry. 'Perhaps, but you must have seemed like the equivalent of the golden goose. And, let's face it, you've gone off-lay.'

He stared at her. 'You know nothing about it.'

'No? Then why don't you tell me? Is the great Chay Buchanan suffering from a terminal case of writer's block?' she demanded. She already knew the answer. He couldn't stop writing, but he would rather not publish than face the publicity. There must be some good reason. . . What exactly did Nigel know? Or suspect? 'I wasn't fooled by that nonsense about a diary,' she continued, a little recklessly. 'And I don't suppose Poppy will be if she takes time to think about it. So what is it? What are you hiding from?' The beautiful face of the girl in the photograph flashed on to her mind's eye. 'What happened to your wife, Chay?'

His face went white beneath the tan. Whether with anger or shock she couldn't tell, but instinctively she held her breath, waiting for the explosion. It never came.

'Maria. . .is dead.'

The painful words fell into a shocked silence so sudden, so complete, that she heard a petal fall from the bunch of yellow daisies she and Tom had picked and put in a jug on the kitchen table.

Sophie drew in a long shuddering breath. 'I'm sorry,' she whispered. 'That was unforgivable of me.'

'You keep doing unforgivable things, Sophie,' he rasped, the hard planes of his cheeks, the fierce hook of his broken nose so close that she could hardly breathe. She lowered her lashes, to block out the pitiless expression.

'You. . .you just seem to bring out the worst in me,' she whispered.

'Do I?' He hooked her chin with his hand, lifted her face to his unsparing scrutiny. It seemed to last forever. 'I wonder what the best is like?'

Defensive, prickly, too aware that his fingers at her throat were making her tremble, she retaliated. 'You're not about to find out.' Still he probed, searched her face, and she panicked. 'Of course, if you let me keep your photographs it would help,' she said, deliberately provoking.

'Would it? In that case I'll have to live with the worst.' And he dropped his hand, turning away, missing her surge of relief as she leaned weakly back against the sink. When he spoke again his tone was once more harsh. 'You'd better come down to the stables with me to fetch Tom; he wants to show you his pony.'

It took a moment to pull her wits together and he glanced impatiently from the doorway. 'I'm coming,' she said quickly.

He led the way out of the kitchen and across the garden and then held open the gate to a narrow path that ran between old drystone walls down the hill towards a group of buildings.

Walking alongside him on the narrow path, his arm brushing against her with every step, was a nightmare. He was so. . .physical. She tried to drop back, but he put his hand on her shoulder, easing her in front of him to give her more room, and he left it there. The nervous tingles from the unintentional contact were suddenly in danger of becoming a solid warm glow.

Sophie fought it. With each step she reminded herself of his insults, every cutting remark, the casual touch of his hands, of his lips used to emphasise his complete mastery over her. She was his prisoner, she reminded herself. And somewhere out there was Nigel, waiting for her to 'kiss and tell'. Already she had enough for Nigel to have a field-day if he continued to demand her co-operation in return for information about her sister. . . She glanced at the man beside her, and felt a deep pit of cold misery in her stomach.

Tom's delighted face, his small hands tugging her away to admire his golden-coated pony, came as a blessed relief. 'She's lovely, Tom. What's her name?'

'Melita. It means honey,' he told her.

'The old Roman name for Malta? How pretty.'

'I call her Melly.'

Sophie rubbed the pony's nose. 'Can you ride her yet?'

'I can ride anything,' he said proudly.

Startled, she turned to Chay. 'Tom's only had Melly a few days,' he said, coming up to them and offering the pony a knob of sugar on the flat of his hand. 'She's a birthday present from his grandmother.' He gave some sugar to Tom, and, taking her arm, led her along the yard to introduce her to the other horses.

'You have a mother?' she murmured in mocking disbelief, as she made a fuss of a gentle-mouthed grey mare.

'You thought, perhaps, that I sprang full-grown from dragon's teeth?'

'I don't think anything,' she said, preferring to keep her thoughts to herself. 'But I know you are quite prepared to keep me here against my will.'

'I'm glad you realise that. Although, as a prison, this

has much to commend it.' His gesture invited her to look around. Tom was laughing as his pony butted him with her nose, wanting more of the sugar he had in his hand. Twany could be heard, singing tunelessly as he worked in the tack-room. Around them a warm, flower-scented evening drew in.

'"The isle is full of noises, Sounds and sweet airs, that give delight, and hurt not. . ."'? Sophie quoted softly. Then she turned to him. 'But it's still a prison, Chay. No matter whether you are locked up, or simply bound to a place by memories.' She forced herself to face him, confront the hard line of his mouth, his shaded eyes. 'I'm sorry I asked about your wife, Chay. You must have loved her very much.'

He didn't answer. He didn't need to. The brief expression of pain that crossed his face was all the answer she needed.

Tom raced up. 'Will you ride with us tomorrow, Sophie?' he begged. 'Please? She could ride Rowan, Papa.'

'I. . .' Words failed her. What could she say to the child?

Chay's hand reached over her head to stroke the beast's neck. 'Do you ride?' he asked abruptly.

'Yes,' she said. 'But it's. . .it's been a while.'

'Yes!' Tom punched the air. Then rushed off to tell Twany.

Chay turned back to the bay. 'We go out very early,' he said. 'We won't wait for you.'

'Aren't you afraid I'll bolt for it?'

His eyes gleamed dangerously. 'You could try,' he offered.

'Why are you keeping me here? Why is it so important?' He didn't answer. 'Please, Chay, let me go.' And instinctively she laid a hand upon his arm.

His face hardened. 'It will take more than a pair of bright eyes to move me, Sophie. I warned you.'

For a moment their eyes held. Then Tom's insistent clamour for her attention broke through, and she let him pull her away to meet Rowan. And when she looked again Chay was striding away across the concrete yard.

So much for her determination to get away. Well, tomorrow was another day. She'd think of something. She had to. And with that promise to herself she surrendered to Tom's enthusiasm.

'When is your birthday, Tom?' she asked, as they walked up the path together half an hour later.

'On Sunday,' he said. 'Do you really think Papa might let me have a party?'

'Why don't you ask him?'

Tom pulled a doubtful face. 'If you asked him for me,' he suggested, 'he might say yes.' He tucked his hand trustingly in hers. 'He likes you.'

Startled, she glanced down at the boy. 'What makes you think that?'

'He ducked you in the pool,' Tom said confidentially. 'You only do that to people you really like.'

She choked back her laughter at this child's-eye-view of friendship. Then she remembered. She had ducked Chay, too.

Sophie was showing Tom the way to make waterspouts in the bath when his shrieks of laughter brought Chay to see what all the excitement was about. His arrival coincided with a particularly tremendous whoosh of water, which erupted over the edge of the bath to splatter a pair of hand-made shoes and well-cut trousers.

'What the devil. . .?'

Before she could stop him, Tom shouted, 'Look, Papa!' and copied her.

Sophie leapt to her feet. 'I'm sorry——'

Chay was staring down at the bath, watching Tom's game. 'Matt and I used to do that. I'd forgotten.'

'Matt?'

'My brother.' He glanced at her. 'We used to compete to see who could make the biggest spouts. The mess we made. . .' He shrugged. 'Matt and I used to compete at everything.' His gaze returned to the child in the bath. 'Stupid.'

'Is it? I used to compete with my sister. Without much success.'

'Used to?' His eyes met hers in sharp query, and she remembered that his brother was dead. 'Not now?'

'No. Not now,' she said, a little shakily. 'We grew up.'

'That was clever of you. Matt never quite got over the fact that he was a year younger than me, the need to prove himself. I suppose I should have let him win occasionally.'

'He would have known,' she said. She had always known, on those rare occasions than Jennie had taken pity on her. 'And it's far worse.'

'How reassuring.' She stared at him. He was angry. What on earth had she said? 'I'm going to change.' He paused. 'If you need anything tonight, Twany lives in the cottage behind the stables.'

A reminder that she was being watched? 'I'll be fine,' she said abruptly. She turned to the boy in the bath. 'Come on, Tom. The water's getting cold. Time to get out.'

'Ask him now, Sophie!' Tom demanded in a loud whisper.

'No, Tom, not now,' she shushed him. Now was not a good time.

But it was too late; he had heard. 'Ask me what?' Chay demanded, turning in the doorway.

Sophie, wrapping Tom in a towel, kept her eyes firmly on the boy. 'Tom seems to think you'll be more likely to agree if I ask you if he can have a birthday party,' she said quickly. Then, because this seemed to imply some criticism, she added, 'I can't think why. I'm sure you'll let him have one.'

There was a long moment of silence and she finally looked up, unaware how her eyes were pleading for the child. Chay regarded her intently, the slightest frown creasing his brow. Then he turned to Tom. 'This was your own idea?'

'Yes,' he said. Then, under his father's searching gaze, he faltered. 'Not exactly.' Chay's glance swivelled back to Sophie, and she flinched at the frostbitten chill that accused her. But Tom hadn't finished. 'Dr Paul said I should have a party, and invite Elena and Michael and little Paul and. . .'

For a moment Chay's eyes continued to challenge Sophie, and for a moment she met him head-on. Then he pulled a face and turned back to Tom. No apology. Well, what did she expect?

'All right,' he said, holding up a hand to halt the excited flow. 'I get the picture. So, you want a party for your birthday?' The child nodded, almost holding his breath. 'What kind of party?'

'One like Uncle Matt had. Grandma told me about it. With cowboys and Indians and a barbecue,' he said, hopping from one leg to the other as he began to believe it was going to be all right. 'On the beach.' He began to rattle off a list of the most desirable food, who should be invited and what games they would play, oblivious to the brief spasm of anguish that crossed his father's face. 'Can I, Papa? Please?'

Chay tucked down until his eyes were level with

Tom's. 'A party means a lot of work. Who's going to arrange all this?'

'Sophie will,' Tom said confidently. He turned and looked up at her. 'You will, Sophie, won't you?'

Chay raised his eyes to meet hers and she was surprised to discover that a glint of amusement had replaced the anger. 'No problem, then. If Sophie is prepared to organise it, Tom, of course you can have a party,' he said. 'But she must decide.'

'But that's not——' Fair. It wasn't fair. But he already knew that. That was what he found so amusing. Because Tom had taken her agreement for granted.

'Yes!' he cried, punching the air, abandoning his towel as he danced about the bathroom. 'Yes! A party! Thank you, Sophie! Thank you, Papa!'

'But it can't be Sunday,' he warned. 'We'll have it on Saturday.'

Tom didn't care. He was having a party. Overwhelmed by the child's excitement, Sophie turned helplessly to Chay as he straightened. 'But I can't,' she said.

'Can't you?' Chay regarded her with an expression that would have provoked a saint. 'You tell him,' he said. Then he turned and walked away.

Sophie took one look at Tom's ecstatic face and knew she couldn't do it. Between them they had her trapped, and she suddenly discovered that there was more than one way to be held prisoner. A fact, she was sure, that Chay was quite well aware of.

'Come on, Tom,' she said, with a trace of a sigh. 'Let's get you into bed.'

She left him compiling a list of friends who must be invited to his birthday party and went downstairs in search of Chay. She found him in the drawing-room. He had changed into a cream linen suit, with a deep blue shirt that seemed to reflect into his eyes, turning their depths from Arctic to Mediterranean, making it very hard to remember how angry she was. He glanced up from the drinks table.

'Would you like something?' he offered.

'A gin and tonic, please,' she said, with feeling. 'That was a bit below the belt, Chay.'

'Oh, quite a long way below,' he agreed, handing her a glass, quite unperturbed by the admission. 'But not quite as low as you rifling through my desk.'

Sophie blushed. 'How did you know?'

'I didn't.' He raised his glass. 'But I do now.'

'Oh!'

'You saw Maria's photograph.' It wasn't a question.

'I was looking for my passport and car keys.' She sipped nervously at her drink. 'She was. . .very beautiful.'

'Yes. She was certainly that.' His eyes had gone blank. He put his glass down with a snap. 'I suppose you saw the manuscript as well. Did you read it?'

'No.'

'I wish you had been as restrained when you decided to spill the beans to Poppy.'

'Since I'm so much trouble, perhaps you should reconsider keeping me here,' she suggested hopefully.

'And disappoint Tom?'

She took a deep breath. 'In that case, Chay,' she said, 'I freely confess to helping myself to some of your notepaper to write to my neighbour.' She produced the letter she had written. 'Would you post it for me? She'll worry if I don't let her know that I've been delayed.'

'Delayed?' He took the letter from her and glanced at the address.' When he looked up his face was lined with suspicion. 'What reason have you given for the. . . delay?'

'I didn't give any reasons. But she looks after my flat, feeds my cat. . .'

'Really? Your cat?' He was deeply sceptical. '"Don't forget to feed Tiddles, and by the way could you send the enclosed to the *Sunday*——?"'

'No!'

'Perhaps you'd care to tell me why I should believe you?'

'No, thank you,' she resolutely declined his offer. 'I don't care to be called a liar.'

'Maybe you could convince me that you're not?'

'With pleasure. Please don't be squeamish, Chay. Just open the letter and read it for yourself,' she instructed coldly. 'I realise that it's not quite in the rifling-through-desk class of prying. But you're pretty good at the handbag variety, so reading other people's mail shouldn't prove so very difficult.' Her grey eyes sparked anger, and for a moment they seemed to hang on the edge. . .

'Papa?'

Chay swung around. 'What are you doing out of bed, Tom?' he snapped.

The boy was clutching a sheet of paper and a pencil. 'I just wanted to ask Sophie. . .'

'Ask Sophie what?'

'Chay!' She crossed to the boy and put her arm around him. 'What is it?' she asked gently.

'I just wanted to ask you,' he half whispered. 'Would your friend like to come to my party?'

Sophie went white. 'Friend?' Chay repeated, his voice dangerously soft. 'What friend, Tom?'

Reassured by his father's gentle tone, Tom relaxed. 'He came yesterday. . .when you were out.'

'Did he?' His eyes met Sophie's over the child's head. 'What was his name?' The question wasn't addressed to Tom.

'It was Nigel,' she said.

'Nigel. Of course. Put him on your list, Tom. I'd very much like to meet. . .Nigel.'

Tom's face creased in concentration. 'How do you spell that?'

'Sophie will tell you later.' He crossed the room and steered Tom through the door. 'Go back to bed now.'

Still concentrating hard, the boy wandered back up the stairs. For a long time after he had gone there was silence.

'Did you think I could just disappear and no one would worry about me?' Sophie finally demanded, unable to bear it a moment longer.

'Why did he assume you would be here?'

'Where else would I be? He was waiting for me to get home. When I didn't turn up he phoned my hotel. I wasn't there either.'

'So? Why didn't you leave with him?'

Because he wouldn't take me. He wants me to stay and have an affair with you and tell him all about it so that he can put it in some sordid magazine. What would he do if she said that? She shuddered. 'Don't you think I wanted to? You have my passport.'

'You could have got a temporary travel document from the High Commission.'

'And my camera.'

'It must be insured.'

'I couldn't have left Tom,' she said a little desperately. 'I didn't know about Twany. . .'

'He'll be back, then?'

She stiffened at the thought of Nigel waiting on Sunday evening. 'No,' she said quickly. 'Why should he bother? I didn't do the job——'

'Damn you!' He thrust the letter into his pocket. 'I ought to have thrown you out, battered and bruised as you were.'

'Then why didn't you?'

'I don't know!' They glared at one another with a deep and mutual antipathy. Then he took a step towards her. 'Yes, I do,' he said, his voice like velvet ripping as he grasped her shoulders and dragged her towards him, his mouth descending in a hard, bruising kiss.

It was as if he hated himself for being unable to resist her. As if he was punishing her for being irresistible. The surprise, the shock of it stunned her. And by the time she realised that she ought to be struggling, making some serious move to stop him, it was very nearly too late.

His hands had slipped from her shoulders to her waist, drawing her into treacherously seductive contact with his thighs, his loins. Her body was already beginning to dissolve, seduced by the warm scent of his skin, melting against him until the soft curves of her body were pressed hard against his body, and she was dangerously close to forgetting that she detested him. Close to forgetting what he had done to her. Close, but not totally lost to sanity. In a moment of blinding anger at his arrogant assumption that he could kiss her without so much as a by-your-leave, and casually reduce her to mindless jelly, she swung her right foot and kicked him, very hard, on the shin.

For a moment the tightening of his grip was the only indication that he had felt anything. Then, with a shuddering sigh, he released her abruptly and stepped back, looking down at his leg as if he couldn't quite believe what had happened. When he looked up his eyes were leaden. 'If you weren't enjoying yourself, Sophie, you only had to say,' he said.

'Enjoying. . .' Hardly able to believe her ears, she exploded. 'Let me tell you that I've enjoyed a visit to the dentist more,' she lied. 'And, as for telling you anything, I ask you to recall that my mouth was otherwise engaged!'

'So it was.' His cool fingers touched her bee-stung mouth, hot and throbbing from his cavalier treatment. 'But for future reference, Sophie, if you simply stop kissing someone back, they usually get the message. There's no need for violence.'

She hadn't! She hadn't kissed him back! How dared he suggest that she had? 'Haven't you got an appointment you're anxious to keep?' she reminded him sharply. 'I'm sure Poppy Curzon will be far more appreciative of your caveman tactics.'

'You may be right.' His voice took on a dangerous edge. 'I'll let you know in the morning.' With that he turned and walked from the room, and a moment later the front door closed somewhat forcefully, making her jump.

For a long breathless moment she stood there, hardly able to believe her ears. Hardly able to believe the sharp bile of jealousy that stung at her throat. 'Poppy Curzon is welcome to you,' she called after him, a little desperately. The hollow echo that came reverberating back to her ears that Poppy Curzon had got him was not a comfort.

She fled to the study. If the key opened the door to the second floor she would be able to lay her escape plans. But when she wrenched the drawer open, the key had gone.

'Sophie!' There was a sickening jolt as her fall was abruptly halted. 'Sophie, wake up.'

She tried to speak, but the fear, the horror of it clammed her mouth, and nothing would come out. Her heart was pounding horribly and she still couldn't believe that she was alive, that Chay was holding her close, rocking her gently, his arms about her and her cheek pressed against the smooth dark silk of his dressing-gown. 'Wake up, now.' His voice was insistent. 'You're safe.'

Safe. She lifted her head and stared up at him. 'It was a dream, wasn't it?'

'More like a nightmare, to judge by the amount of noise you were making,' he said softly.

She was trembling with the sickening sensation that still clutched at her. 'I was falling and falling. . .' She shuddered. 'It was horrible.'

'Do you often have nightmares?'

'Not like that.' Not real, screaming nightmares. Only endless exhausting dreams in which she searched hopelessly for her sister. She shuddered again. 'Never like that.'

He held her away from him and looked at her. 'Come on. Downstairs. I'll warm you some milk.'

Something in his eyes alerted her to the dangerous intimacy of being held by him like this, on her bed in the middle of the night. 'No.' She drew back a little. 'I'll be all right,' she said, with an attempt at brightness, then spoiled the effect by shivering convulsively. Still, somewhere in the dark recesses of her mind, she was plunging down that endless cliff-face.

'The minute you close your eyes, it'll start all over again,' he warned her. 'Believe me. I know,' he added with conviction. He looked around, took her wrap from behind the door and held it out for her. 'You'll have to wake up properly before you can go back to sleep.'

No need to throw back the quilt, she noticed dimly. It had fallen to the floor in her agitation, leaving her covered only by her brief two-piece sleepsuit, an oyster satin camisole and matching French knickers that left precious little to the imagination. She swung her legs to the floor and dived into the wrap, tying it firmly around her.

'I'm sorry that I disturbed you,' she muttered, keeping her eyes firmly diverted from the short silk dressing-gown tied carelessly about his waist, under which she was fairly certain he was naked.

'I wasn't asleep.' He placed his hand firmly at her back and propelled her from the room and down the stairs. 'Come on.' She glanced at him as she opened the kitchen door.

'Why can't you sleep?'

He took a carton of milk from the refrigerator and poured it into a saucepan and set it to heat. 'I said that I wasn't asleep, not that I couldn't.'

'But. . .it's three o'clock in the morning.' Then bright colour spread across her cheeks. 'Oh!' She reached hurriedly for a mug to cover her confusion. Poppy had clearly welcomed him with open arms.

He took the mug from her. 'I posted your letter.'

'Then you read it?'

He didn't answer. 'You didn't write to your parents. Won't they worry too?' he asked, carefully pouring out the milk and handing it to her.

She sipped, not wanting to discuss her relationship with her parents. 'I don't live at home. They don't know where I am from day to day.'

'You mentioned a sister? What about her?'

'Jennie.' She felt suddenly hollow with longing. 'We're identical twins.'

'Identical. . . Lord help us, there are two of you?'

'I'm afraid so.' For just a moment her eyes responded to the unexpected smile. Then they clouded. 'At least, we *were* identical.'

'Were?'

'I haven't seen Jennie for nearly seven years. She ran away from home when she was seventeen.'

'Ran away?' He was clearly shocked. Angry, almost. 'Why?'

Her lips tightened at his disapproval. What could he possibly know of such things, shut away in his private world? 'It's a common enough story,' she told him, defences slamming up, but too late. 'She got involved with a man my parents disapproved of. Then when she became pregnant he left her to face the music alone.'

'But your parents? Were they so harsh?' he demanded, and she glanced up to find herself the object of a pair of deeply questing eyes. It seemed oddly important to him.

'No. They were never harsh with her.' On the contrary. The only thing they had ever tried to deny her had driven her away. 'They loved Jennie. They would have done anything for her. That's why she ran. She knew how badly she had behaved,' she replied, quickly dropping her lids to disguise the sharp sting of tears glistening in her eyes. She had seen her parents age while they had privately grieved for their beautiful daughter who, rather than bear their imagined reproach, had taken her wounded pride and disappeared without a trace. And she had been unable to comfort them. The mirror image of their lost child, they couldn't stand to have her near them. And soon afterwards she too had left.

Now she had been given a chance to reunite them. All it had needed was a photograph of Chay Buchanan and she had blown it. Except that Nigel had given her another chance. If she could get a little gossip—a scrap of dirt. . . And there *was* something. She knew it. Tied up in the story of a dead wife, a motherless child and a writer who couldn't stand publicity.

She stared into the mug. Why else was she here? His prisoner? Sitting in this silent, night-time kitchen, drinking warm milk and recovering from a nightmare with a man who she knew she should loathe? But didn't. No matter how hard she tried. She stood up abruptly and crossed to the sink to rinse her mug. Well, she would just have to try harder. For Jennie's sake.

'Leave it,' he instructed, coming behind her and taking it. For a moment his long, strong fingers entwined with hers, a gentle gesture that for once appeared to offer no threat. She glanced up at him over her shoulder, about to protest that she was quite capable of doing it herself, but as their eyes met the words died in her throat. His look was fathoms deep and for a moment neither of them moved.

'I think I'd better go back to bed,' she said quickly, and wondered if that breathless little sound had really come from her. 'Thank you. . .for coming to. . .' She hesitated, unable to think of a word that would exactly cover the circumstances.

'To what?'

'To help,' she offered, with a little lift of the chin.

'Any time, Sophie. In fact, it's getting to be quite a habit.'

'A habit!' She repeated her words out loud as she lay in her bed. Anyone would think she was her own personal disaster area.

Despite his instruction to sleep, for a long time Sophie lay wakeful in the dark, forcing herself to remember just what had driven her over the edge of that cliff in a boiling red haze of rage. Making herself hate him.

CHAPTER SEVEN

CHAY's hand on her shoulder brought Sophie instantly awake, and she opened her eyes to find his dark tousled head above her. 'It's time to get up,' he said abruptly.

The light was pearl-soft. It was still very early and she was certain it was only a moment since she had closed her eyes. She groaned, remembering Tom's eagerness that she ride with him. 'What time is it?'

'You don't want to know that.'

'It's that early?'

'It'll be worth it,' he said crisply, as if he too regretted the closeness of their late-night tryst; as if he had also spent the intervening hours reminding himself just what had brought them together.

She struggled to sit up. 'Is that a promise?' she asked, smothering a yawn.

'You have my absolute guarantee. But you have just five minutes to get ready if you want to catch the sunrise from the ridge.'

'Five minutes?' She regarded him with rather less than amusement. 'As long as that? I could be ready for a party in five minutes.'

'Now, that I would pay to see,' he said, as she swung her feet to the floor, then Sophie blushed wide awake as she realised that she was freely offering him more of an eyeful than was entirely sensible in the circumstances. She made a grab for the cover and quickly hauled it up to her chin.

'What about Tom?' she asked sharply. 'Is he up?'

'He's downstairs having breakfast. We'll see you down at the stables. In five minutes.'

The second the door closed behind him she dashed to the bathroom to splash her face with cold water to finish the job of waking up. Then, pulling a soft cream shirt and a comfortable pair of dark red trousers from the wardrobe, she dressed quickly. It had not been an idle boast when she had said she could be ready for anything in five minutes. She had spent a year as a junior photographer on a provincial newspaper, where she had rapidly learned that if you didn't move fast, you didn't get your picture.

Chay straightened from adjusting Tom's stirrups as she hurried into the stable-yard and turned away to fetch a hard hat for her. 'Here.' He jammed it on her head. 'If you come off, it's like hitting concrete.' He fastened the hat beneath her chin, apparently unaware that his fingers were an exquisite torture against her neck. Or maybe he wasn't. Something seemed to happen to her skin whenever he touched it. It seemed to spark under his touch, come alive. Something he could hardly fail to be aware of. So much for her middle-of-the-night determination to keep a safe yard of distance between them.

The moment he had finished she turned away to make a fuss of Rowan, using the excuse of getting acquainted with the horse to cover the need to get her breathing back under control.

'Come on, Sophie, up you get,' he said impatiently, and she turned and placed her foot in his linked hands. He threw her up into the saddle, then adjusted the stirrups for her. She gathered in the reins and mur-mured a few crooning words in Rowan's ear as she walked her around the yard. Chay gave her a long hard look, then, apparently satisfied that she knew what she was doing, he mounted the huge bay gelding. 'Lead on, Tom,' he said.

Tom trotted confidently off, and Sophie watched

with considerable admiration. 'I thought he only got Melly a day or two ago?' she asked.

'She's not his first pony. His grandmother put him on a Shetland as soon as he could stand. Her own career as a three-day-eventer was cut short by an accident, but she's determined to have a Buchanan in the Olympic team. Since Matt and I refused to co-operate, she's turned her attention to Tom.'

'With some success, apparently.'

'We'll see. I was pretty keen until I reached my teens, but once I bought my first motorbike. . .' He shrugged.

She glanced at him, trying to imagine what he must have looked like astride a bike in close-fitting black leathers. Dangerous. 'And Matt?' she asked quickly.

'Once Matt discovered that girls love to be around horses he did spend an awful lot of time at the stables.' He grinned unexpectedly. 'But I'm afraid not very much of it was on a horse.'

'What. . .? Oh!'

He laughed as she blushed, then reached across and caught her arm. 'There, look.' As they crested the ridge and came alongside Tom the sun was rising, dripping gold, from the fairy-tale blue of the sea. They sat and watched in silence as the dark rocks and barren landscape turned to butter and honey about them.

'I think,' she murmured at last, 'that was the most beautiful sunrise I've ever seen.' But then everything seemed more focused since she had met Chay Buchanan. New-washed and crystal-bright.

The bay moved restlessly and they began to move on, walking the horses along the ridgeway path. 'You say that as if you'd seen the sun rise a hundred times. Do you make a habit of getting up before dawn?' Chay asked.

'I've been up before dawn working every day since I

came to Malta. It goes with the job. Sunrises over power stations, over sea-fronts, over municipal buildings, hotels—especially hotels, because there are fewer people about. I even took a photograph of that new hotel your company built. . .' Even as the words left her mouth she knew she had made a mistake.

'You have been busy,' he said, with just a touch of acid. 'What a pity you couldn't bring your camera with you today. You could have added "Sunrise over Chay Buchanan" to complete your portfolio.' Underlying the even tone there was steel in his voice, and suddenly the beauty of the morning turned to ashes.

'There's not enough light for a portrait,' she responded miserably. 'I hate using flash for faces.'

'I'm sure you could have forced yourself.'

'Whether I could have or not is surely all rather academic? You are not about to sit still while I take a photograph of you, at sunrise or any other time. Are you?'

'No, I'm not. But I very much doubt that you've forgotten why you're here. You're just biding your time, hoping that I will.'

He turned the bay gelding on to a path already taken by Tom, who hadn't been interested enough in the sunrise to linger. 'Stay close,' he warned, as he spurred the horse into a brisk canter.

Sophie almost laughed out loud. Did he really think she was crazy enough to try and escape on horseback? The hills were mined with old rabbit-warrens. One careless footstep and he would be forced to come to her aid yet again. Twice was more than enough.

She followed at a sedate trot, unwilling to risk life and limb on the unknown path, but as she approached a fork in the track Chay was waiting for her. Perfectly still, horse and man as one, looking out to sea. Only a playful breeze whipped up a lock of dark hair and winnowed the bay's mane to betray that the pair were not some lost heroic statue. Then he turned and the illusion evaporated.

'If you want me close, you'll have to slow down,' she said, trotting up alongside him.

'I thought you could ride,' he said witheringly. But he kept his impatient mount at walking pace as they waded, knee-deep at times, in acres of narcissus and euphorbia and blue borage. The next hour passed, it seemed to Sophie, with the speed of light, as he pointed out landmarks, including another tower, abandoned and crumbling, on a distant headland, built, he told her, by the knights to guard against the marauding galleys of their enemies.

Tom, who had trotted ahead most of the way, had dismounted and was waiting impatiently for them at the cliff-top path.

When he saw him, Chay swore softly and, tossing his reins to Sophie, swung from the saddle and strode across to the boy.

'Come away from there,' he commanded.

'But I wanted to show Sophie,' he said, his high voice carrying to her on the breeze. 'I wanted to tell her that this is where you and Uncle Matt used to race one another up the cliff. See,' he said. 'It's almost *exactly* where she was stuck.' And he pointed, too excited to see the shock whiten his father's face. He turned away from the edge and ran across to Sophie. 'Uncle Matt and Papa used to race each other up the cliff-face at the beginning of every summer holidays. Grandma told me. Come and look.' He tugged at her hand.

Grandma, Sophie thought privately, as she slipped from the saddle, must have been mad. The boy clearly couldn't wait to try it for himself. 'They must have been a lot older than you,' she observed, forcing her voice to remain calm, even though her entire body seemed to be trembling at the thought of him climbing down that dreadful rockface.

'Papa was ten and Uncle Matt was nine,' he said proudly.

'You've a few years before you try, then,' she said, trying to keep her voice a great deal calmer than she was feeling at the thought of his small, infinitely fragile body being battered against those rocks. 'Even Uncle Matt waited until he was nine,' she reminded him.

But his face was set in a dangerously truculent expression at the thought of waiting. 'I'm going to do it before then,' he said, with determination.

Sophie glanced across at Chay, who was rigid with shock as he stared at the boy. 'I think you'd better go back to the stables, Tom,' she said quickly. 'Twany will help you with Melly.' She gave him a leg up and watched for a moment as he trotted down the hill. Then she tethered the two horses to a nearby bush and walked across to Chay.

'I had no idea he knew. She must have told him when she was over here for Easter. It explains the sudden interest. . .' He sank on to a rock. 'I cannot believe that my mother could be so stupid. To fill his head with such rubbish.'

'He seems to set a lot of store by what his Uncle Matt did,' Sophie said carefully, as she lowered herself beside him.

'My mother is always telling Tom stories about the things Matt used to get up to, and heaven knows there's plenty to tell. But this. . .' He turned to her. 'How could she?'

'Because she missed him.' Her parents talked about Jennie all the time. Not how clever she was, or how pretty, but the crazy things she had done. The endless times they had been called to school to listen to the

Head's complaints about her wildness. The hours they had waited for the police to find them when Jennie had insisted they must prove themselves by spending the night in a deserted house. . . As if, by recalling the times when it had all turned out happily, they might make it happen again. She shook the thought away. 'What happened to him, Chay?'

'He. . .fell.'

'Fell?' She stared at him in growing horror as she followed his blank stare. 'Down there?'

His face was bleak as he stared out at the sea. 'It was the best part of seven years ago. The twenty-seventh of October.'

'What was he doing on the cliff?' she asked. 'The pair of you must surely have grown out of such craziness by then?'

'Must we?' he replied tersely. Then, realising that this was hardly an explanation, he shrugged. 'We'd been coming to Malta for the summer holidays for as long as I can remember. Dad was in the Navy, based here in Malta at one time. He bought a long lease on the tower and did it up as a holiday base. "Doing the cliff" became a part of the holiday. A nightmare to overcome before you could enjoy the weeks of freedom.'

'I don't understand. . .'

'You can get to the bottom of the cliff from the beach, if you climb over a few rocks and don't mind getting a bit wet. There's a cave there and one day we'd been exploring it. When it was time to go back Matt challenged me to climb out. I told him he was mad, but Matt said I was just scared, and set off on his own. I was older, responsible for him, so I couldn't let him go on his own.' His mouth tightened. 'And I was damned if I was going to let him beat me.' He glanced at her with a little start, almost as if he had forgotten she was there and he was talking to himself. 'I should have done, of course. Then it would all have been over.'

'And he would have crowed all summer,' she said, her warm grey eyes deep with understanding

'It shouldn't have mattered, Sophie.'

'When you're ten years old, Chay, you don't know that.'

He stared at her with something like surprise that she should understand. 'I suppose not. Anyway, that was the start of it. Stupid, dangerous, intensely competitive. Looking back, I'm amazed that neither of us had been killed, or at the very least seriously hurt, before.'

'Why didn't your parents stop you?' Sophie asked in amazement.

'Father died when I was nine, in a car accident, and Mother didn't know we were doing it. At least, not at first, and when she found out she just laughed. It proved we were strong and gutsy. She liked that. Matt took his dare-devil madness from her. And, anyway, it had become a sort of ritual, the first thing we did when we came back every year.'

'But surely you weren't *still* doing it?' she asked. The very thought of a world-renowned novelist risking his life in such a manner was surreal.

'No. I hadn't been to Malta in three or four years. But Matt was living here then. Running a wind-surfing club in summer, painting in the winter.' He glanced across at her. 'Those panels in the bedroom are his.'

'They are very beautiful,' she said quietly.

He searched her face, saw that she meant it and nodded. 'I'd won some literary prize that year and the whole world wanted me. I'd been doing the lecture circuit—the States, Australia, the Far East. I don't know how many thousands of miles I covered. I wrote to ask Matt if I could come for a couple of months before starting the new book.' He caught her questioning look and shrugged. 'A courtesy. We bought the lease jointly from Mother when she decided the tower was too much to cope with, but it was Matt's home. When I arrived he was in a really stupid mood. On a sort of high. I should have recognised the symptoms; he was always like that when he had a secret.' He paused. 'I'd been travelling for the best part of twenty-four hours and all I wanted was to crash out, but Matt had other ideas. I had hardly stepped over the threshold before he threw down the challenge to "do the cliff".

'I told him to forget it. Neither of us had climbed the thing in five years, and I was certainly in no shape to attempt it. But he wouldn't let it rest. He said I wouldn't do it because I knew he could beat me. I told him to consider it a fact.'

Sophie felt her heart turn over with pity. She knew what it was like to be the one always following in her brilliant sister's footsteps. 'He must have been very jealous of you,' she said, with feeling.

'I don't think I had realised how much until then. The stupid thing was that I had always envied him his ability to paint. I had offered to arrange an exhibition. . .but he reckoned his pictures would only sell as curiosities because he was my brother. He was wrong.'

He was quiet for a long time and Sophie said nothing, remembering her own dogged determination to copy everything her sister did, and Jennie cruelly leading her into dangers she had been ill-equipped to deal with. She had broken her leg the year they were sixteen, putting her horse to an impossibly high fence that Jennie had cleared with ease. She had spent months with her leg in plaster, coming to terms with the truth that it could just as easily have been her neck. She had grown up that summer, and when her sister had gone on to play new and even more dangerous games she had finally been able to resist the temptation to play follow-my-leader. But she had always blamed herself for not being there when her sister had needed her.

'Did you climb it with him?' she asked eventually, to blot out unhappy thoughts of her own.

He too seemed to come back from a long distance inside his head. 'No. The fact that I simply didn't care was like waving a red rag in front of a bull. He was determined to show me. And he was good. He was fit from wind-surfing all summer. The only exercise I'd had was flapping my mouth. Then, just before the ledge, he seemed to get stuck, and shouted for me to come and give him a hand.' Chay's skin was a sickly grey. 'I. . .I thought he was just fooling. Trying to get me on to the cliff-face so that he could race on and beat me. By the time I realised and tried to reach him it was too late. I just wasn't fast enough. . .'

He stood up abruptly and crossed to the edge, and stared down into the abyss. Feeling slightly sick, Sophie watched him. Then, to her relief, he turned away and walked back to the horses and freed the reins. She felt bitter shame at the horror he must have felt when he saw her perched upon the ledge. She wanted to say how sorry she was, but his expression did not invite the unburdening of her own guilt.

But there was something. 'Chay?' she said, as they made their way down the hill.

'What is it?'

'Does Tom know how. . .?' She stopped as something clicked in her brain.

'How Matt died?' he finished for her. 'No,' he said, then, as he saw her brow furrowed in deep concentration, he frowned. 'I'll tell him what happened when he's old enough to understand.'

'He's very headstrong. I'm not sure you've time to let him grow up. I believe you should tell him as soon as possible,' she advised.

'Do you? And do you suggest I include the part where I was too stupid to see that Matt was in trouble until it was too late to help?' he demanded harshly.

Her heart almost broke for him. Impulsively she reached across to touch his hand. 'Don't blame yourself for what happened. Matt knew the risk.' So had Jennie. The words jumped into her brain. Jennie had chosen to live dangerously. She could come home any time she wanted to. All it took was courage.

'Matt never considered the risk in anything,' he said coldly. Then he turned to her, and she flinched at the chill in his eyes. 'And I seem to be developing the same careless habit. The longer I keep you here, the more you learn about me, my family.'

'Then perhaps you should let me go right now.'

'No. After next weekend it won't matter. You'll stay until then.'

She was still washing up the breakfast things when there was a ring at the doorbell.

Chay answered it and came back with an attractive woman, somewhere in her late thirties. 'Here you are, Gian, this is Sophie,' Chay introduced her. 'You can see for yourself that I'm not working her to death.'

'Chay!' Gian protested. 'I never said——'

'Gian is Paul Manduca's wife, Sophie. I believe he's sent her to check up on me.'

'What utter nonsense,' she retorted, taking Sophie's hastily wiped hand. 'How are you? Quite recovered from your fall, I hope?' Sophie was aware that Chay was extracting a certain sardonic amusement from the way Gian was sizing her up, trying to work out precisely what their relationship was.

'I'm fine now, thank you,' Sophie reassured the woman. 'I could leave any time,' she added pointedly.

'But I understood that you were staying for a while?'

'You understood correctly, Gian,' Chay intervened smoothly.

'I'm so glad. Theresa is wonderful, of course, but getting on. She was Maria's nurse, you know.' She looked quickly at Chay, clearly afraid that she had said something indiscreet. But there was no reaction beyond a slight tightening of his jaw that only the closest watcher would have detected. 'Tom needs someone younger around him. And that's the reason for my call.' She turned to Chay. 'I do wish you would get a telephone installed, Chay, it would make invitations so much easier.'

Chay's expression suggested that he was not impressed by this argument. 'You can always call me at my office.'

'But you're not at your office, Chay,' she pointed out, and turned back to Sophie. 'I'm taking the children out this afternoon for a treat before the school holidays end, and I wondered if you and Tom would like to join us? I know how busy Chay always is. At least——' she glanced a little shyly at him '—he is usually busy. But since he's not working today, maybe you have something else planned?' She arched a dark questioning brow.

'No, nothing at all.' Sophie studiously avoided Chay's eyes, certain they would contain a warning. 'And I'm sure Tom would love to have some other children to play with,' she said. 'Where are you thinking of going?'

'Nothing too exciting. A boat trip round the harbour, perhaps, and then ices in Sliema.'

'If you'd like a boat trip, Gian, why don't you let me take you out? I'm sure we could find somewhere more entertaining than a tourist trip around the habour,' Chay intervened.

Gian turned to him in surprise. 'Oh, but, Chay, the children love it, and besides, you will be so bored with just women and children for company,' she protested.

'Nonsense. I can't think of any company more charming. Sophie will make us a picnic and we'll go over to Comino and swim in the lagoon. What do you say, Sophie?'

She chose to ignore his infuriatingly smug expression at having checked any opportunity to stray from his control with such ease. 'That sounds like fun,' she agreed. 'I haven't had a chance to swim in the blue lagoon.' She smiled with her teeth. 'Only take photographs.'

'You have a camera?' Gian asked with interest. 'Will you bring it and take some photographs of the children for us?' She pulled a face. 'I'm hopeless. I always manage to cut off the important bits whenever I try.'

'Sophie's camera is out of action, Gian.'

'Oh, what a pity,' Gian said, then brightened. 'It doesn't matter, I'll bring mine along.'

Aware of Chay's eyes narrowing dangerously, Sophie quickly moved on to the subject of the picnic. 'Now, is there anything your children don't like to eat?' she asked.

'Very little,' Gian assured her with feeling, and, after a few moments discussing arrangements for the afternoon, she left.

'Don't get any smart ideas about taking a photograph of me or Tom,' Chay warned as Sophie returned to the kitchen, having seen the other woman to her car.

'I'm fresh out of smart ideas,' she snapped, 'or I wouldn't be here.'

'Maybe. But, just in case, I shall take the films to have them developed.'

'Whatever you say,' she agreed sweetly. 'I'm sure Gian will appreciate the gesture.' Then, rather more tartly, she added, 'I do hope you're getting a good discount for bulk.' She didn't wait for his reply, but turned her attention to the preparation of the picnic, slamming the food angrily upon the table.

'Are you cross with me, Sophie?' Tom asked.

She had been so wound up with temper that she hadn't noticed Tom's huge eyes. 'Oh, Tom. No, darling.' She put her arm around him and hugged him. 'Come and help me get the picnic ready.' And a few minutes later she breathed a huge sigh of relief as she heard the front door close behind Chay as he left for the yacht club to fetch the boat.

Chay was already down at the boat, packing away the food when Gian arrived with her children just after two o'clock, and she was not alone.

'Sophie, this is Cesare. My little brother. He flew in this morning so I brought him along. I hope you don't mind.'

Gian's brother was hardly little. He didn't quite have the stature or maturity of Chay, but he had the 'knock 'em dead' good looks of so many young Italian men. And he clearly knew it. He immediately stepped forward and took Sophie's hand very tenderly in his.

'Sophie,' he murmured, dripping Latin charm. 'What a beautiful name.'

Sophie caught her lower lip between her teeth in an effort to stifle a giggle. 'Of course I don't mind, Gian,' she said. But she wondered what Chay's reaction would be.

'I thought he would be company for Chay,' Gian added, looking around. 'Where is he?'

'Down at the boat. We'd better join him.'

Tom led the way, leaping down steps that had been hewn from the living rock to the small jetty that lay adjacent to a delightfully sheltered curve of beach nestling beneath the tower. Gian followed, leading her youngest by the hand, and Cesare insisted upon taking Sophie's arm and helping her down.

As he swung the children aboard, Chay's impassive gaze followed them along the jetty and Sophie profoundly wished that Cesare would stop treating her like a piece of precious china.

'Cesare,' Chay acknowledged the man briefly. 'Good to see you. Will you get the rope?'

'*Scusi*. . .' he murmured, as with the utmost reluctance he surrendered her hand to go to the front of the boat.

Chay hadn't given any indication as to the type of boat he owned, but if Sophie had had the time to wonder about it, she would have assumed something sleek and expensive, rather like the car he had driven away in earlier in the day. Certainly not the workman-like vessel that was tied up alongside the jetty. A decommissioned Navy patrol boat, it hardly came into the usual category of rich men's toys.

'Not quite what you were expecting?' he asked, apparently able to read her mind with disconcerting ease and amused at what he found there.

'On the contrary,' she snapped back. 'It's fast and dangerous. Exactly like its owner.'

He held out his hand to help her and she had little choice but to lean briefly on him as she jumped down, but as she tried to withdraw her fingers his hand closed fast around them. 'I'm very glad you realise that, Sophie Nash,' he murmured, so softly that only she could hear. 'It would be a mistake to underestimate me. Or to think you have found a champion.' His eyes strayed to the figure impatiently holding the rope at the fore.

She raised her brows a fraction. She hadn't thought of Cesare as a champion. He caught her look. 'I'm not fooled by those innocent grey eyes of yours, Sophie. But Cesare might be. He doesn't know you the way I do.'

'You don't know me, Chay.'

'I'll be the judge of that. Help Gian to fasten these, will you?' he said, thrusting a pile of orange lifejackets at her, and retired to the wheelhouse. 'Let her go, Cesare,' he called.

Gian's children, slightly in awe of Chay, were quiet on the journey, but the moment they were set free to splash in the warm, turquoise-blue water they forgot their shyness and the noise-level rose dramatically.

The children swam for a while in the brilliant water, only Gian's little two-year-old needing armbands. When they had had enough they flopped on to the beach, and Gian produced sun-block and proceeded to cover her children with it. Sophie followed suit, rubbing some of her own on to Tom's shoulders, despite his squirming protestations that he didn't like it.

'Be still, Tom,' Sophie warned him. 'You don't want to burn.'

'It's goopy,' Tom answered, pulling a face. 'You don't have cream on your back.'

'Of course I do,' she replied firmly.

Cesare dropped to his knees beside her. 'May I do this for you?' he said. 'Your skin is so fair. You must be careful not to burn.'

About to say that she had covered herself with sun-block before leaving the house, she caught Chay's warning look.

'Thank you, Cesare,' she said, handing him the bottle with a smile. 'If you could just rub a little on my back.' And she lifted the heavy weight of her hair and twisted it and held it to her crown, her arms provocatively raised.

Gian called, and Tom took his chance to escape and play with the other children, leaving her to suffer the tender ministrations of Cesare, under Chay's menacing eye.

'The straps, *cara*. . .' he murmured apologetically, as he smoothed the cream into her shoulders. 'They are. . .in the way.' She wondered just how many times he had used that helpless little boy technique to ease down a bathing suit that was 'in the way'.

'It's all right,' she said quickly.

'Nonsense,' Chay intervened, throwing a dark shadow between herself and the sun. 'You must protect yourself properly. Here. Give it to me.' Cesare hesitated for a moment, then reluctantly surrendered the sun-block to the imperious hand. 'Your sister needs a little help,' he said, and Cesare was effectively dismissed. He turned and walked stiffly away and Sophie felt rather sorry for him.

'That was unkind,' Sophie chided.

'No, it wasn't. You were being unkind.' And she gasped as he jerked down the soft wide straps of her swimsuit to leave her shoulders quite naked. Then his long, sensitive fingers began to smooth the cool cream into the nape of her neck.

For the past four days, whenever she had been in his company, she had been aware of her body in a way that was new and rather frightening. It was as if the air between them was a conductor, carrying a tiny current of electricity from him to charge her skin and make it tingle.

Now his touch, gentle as a butterfly's kiss, concentrated that charge, and her eyes closed tight and her hands curled into clenched little fists as she fought back the urgent need to complain when his hands moved away from their teasing caress of the skin at her nape. Then the flat of his palm stroked a broad path across her shoulders, before sliding down her back to coat her warm skin with the cream, and she was unable to prevent a gentle sigh escaping her lips.

'Back done,' he said, and she twisted around on the warm sand to face him.

'Thank you,' she offered, a little unsteadily, reaching for her cream.

But he refused to surrender it. 'I haven't finished.' She watched, mesmerised, as he tipped the cream on to his fingers. Then he reached out, and in one fluid movement smoothed it into her throat and down the gentle rise of her breasts until the top of her swimsuit brought him to a halt. For a moment she thought he wouldn't stop there, would simply push the soft fabric away to reveal the tight buds thrusting eagerly against her suit. And the warmth she felt was nothing to do with the sun. It came from deep inside her, forcing her to acknowledge that she wanted him to do that more than anything else in the world.

'Chay.' She murmured his name, closing her eyes, quite lost to shame. It was madness to let him touch her like this. But a quite delightful madness.

'Now it's my turn,' he said, and her eyes snapped wide open as the derisory edge to his voice brought her back from the brink. . .

'You don't need sun-block,' she said quickly, her voice not quite her own. 'You're too dark to burn.'

'It doesn't do to be careless,' he reminded her softly, taking her hand and squeezing cream into the palm. 'Shoulders first, I think, don't you? Make a thorough job of it—I want Cesare to be quite sure that you're unavailable.'

And he presented her with his straight, well-muscled

back and waited. It was agony. She wanted to touch him, stroke him, smooth her hands over his skin. But she was angry too. After a moment he turned his head.

'A man could burn while you're thinking about it,' he said.

'Is that so?' She slapped the cream on to his back, taking some satisfaction from making him jump for a change, rubbing vigorously in all directions, determined not to let her mind know what her hands were thinking as they plied his warm skin and felt the muscle-packed flesh contract beneath her fingers. But his skin was like warm silk, and her hand gradually slowed to a gentle caress as a delicious languor seemed to seep through her body. 'Can I have some more cream?' she asked. Then looked up, to find herself being regarded with disconcerting intensity.

'I think you've had quite enough for a public place,' he said, rising to his feet and dropping the bottle beside her. Then he walked into the water. Angrily she tugged the straps of her costume back into place, glaring at him as he sliced vigorously through the water. Then, realising what he had said, horrified at her own lack of self-control, she looked around, expecting to be the object of a row of dark, accusing eyes.

CHAPTER EIGHT

THE beach was deserted. Sophie leapt to her feet in a sudden panic. Where on earth had everyone disappeared to? Then she caught a glimpse of Gian and Cesare, their hands full of ice-cream cones, as, Pied Piper-like, they made their way down to the cove with an eager band of children at their heels.

She hurried to help. 'I'm sorry, Gian,' she said. 'I would have come with you if you'd said. . .'

'You were busy. And Cesare helped,' she said, handing out the cones to the children and warning them not to drop them in the sand. She glanced at the figure in the water. 'Could you eat two? I'm afraid that Chay's will have run to liquid by the time he's. . . cooled off,' she continued innocently.

As good as her word, Gian had brought along her camera and a couple of films. Sophie took a number of shots of the children paddling and playing a game of French cricket that Chay organised. Cesare kept his distance, restricting himself to long, passionate glances when he thought Chay wasn't looking.

As they settled down for tea she began to snap away at them to use up the remainder of the second roll. Tom turned to Chay to offer him an apple. As she focused on the boy Chay leaned into the shot. It was so natural, so charming a scene, that she had taken it before she had time to consider the wisdom of defying him. For a moment she held her breath, but he hadn't noticed, and she quickly moved the camera on to a safer target. But he had not forgotten his warning and when they were packing up Chay picked up the films.

'Give them to me,' Gian said firmly, scooping them from his hand before he could prevent her. 'I have to go into town tomorrow. It only takes a day to get them developed, you know. I'll get you copies of any that you want.'

For just a moment Chay hesitated, but he made no objection, simply shrugged. 'Fine. Bring them over when you come to the party on Saturday. We'll have a look then.'

'How are the preparations going?' she asked.

'I've barely started,' Sophie confessed. 'I'll have to make the cake tomorrow.'

Gian grinned sympathetically. 'Shall I take Tom home with me?' she offered. 'He can spend the day with us tomorrow and give you a clear run at it. You can come over in the evening to collect him and have supper with us.'

'I know he'd love to,' Sophie said, but doubted that Chay would let his little gaoler out of her sight.

She was wrong. 'Sounds like a good idea, if it's not too much for you, Gian?'

'I won't notice another one,' she laughed. 'Cesare can help. And Paul's home tomorrow. He's got a long weekend.'

'Then tell him to save Saturday to give me a hand, will you? He has more experience of dealing with vast quantities of children than I have.'

'How many are you expecting?'

'Hundreds,' Chay said.

'Sixteen,' Sophie amended. 'His entire class at school, apparently. And your children, of course.'

'Then we'll both come early and give you a hand,' Gian promised.

'Won't you bring Cesare?' she asked, unable to resist annoying Chay. The younger man's eyes brightened at this encouragement.

'I have to return to duty, Saturday night,' he murmured. 'But perhaps dinner, this evening. . .?'

She shook her head quickly, hoping that Chay hadn't heard.

After they had all gone it suddenly seemed very quiet. It made Sophie nervous. She had suggested that Tom was an inadequate chaperon. But when he was there she felt. . .safer. But after her reaction when Chay had covered her with the sun-block. . .

'I'm going to take the boat back to the marina and pick up the car,' Chay said, as she was clearing away the picnic debris. 'You'd better come with me.'

'What's this? Parole?'

'I'll feel safer with you under my eye. I'm certainly not leaving you here to keep an assignation with Cesare.'

'I haven't. . .'

He made a dismissive gesture. 'I saw that little whispered interchange before they left. What did you arrange?'

'Nothing!'

'No? You're very edgy.'

'How kind of you to notice. What a pity you are less astute about the reason.'

His forehead creased in a frown. 'It makes no difference. Cesare will think of some excuse to return.'

She glared at him. 'I have to organise dinner.'

'We'll eat out,' he snapped. 'Can you be ready in half an hour?' He held up a hand before she could protest. 'My apologies. I forgot, temporarily, that in five minutes you can be ready for anything.'

'But not twice in one day.' And she stormed up to her room to stand under a cool shower until her skin tingled and she had regained control of her temper. Although as she dried herself she acknowledged with a certain wryness that the touch of one man had more to do with the way her body glowed than the effects of the sun and the needle-sharp shower together.

She dropped the towel and turned to the mirror, lifting her hand hesitantly to her breast. She drew her fingers lightly across the slight swell of her cleavage, wondering what it would be like to be crushed naked against his chest, to be made love to by a man like Chay Buchanan. Gian had seen Chay's response to Cesare and misunderstood. She had thought that by whisking Tom away for the night she was conspiring to aid romance. Offering two adults who desired each other the perfect end to the perfect day. And it would have been. She knew that. If only it were that simple.

How pleased Nigel would be if he knew how well his perverted little plan was going. The thought sickened her. Because between the nightmare, when she had woken in his arms, and this moment, something had happened. She didn't quite know what. Only that one perfect night with Chay Buchanan would almost certainly break her heart.

She shook her head and, realising with a shock how the time was flying by, grabbed her hair-drier.

She made it with a minute to spare, flying down the stairs, only to come to an abrupt halt two steps up as she saw that he was waiting for her, staring somewhere into space, his hands thrust deep into the pockets of his trousers. He turned as he heard her, and paused for just a moment. And, just for a moment, the dangerous thrill as she caught the widening of his eyes was worth the effort she had made.

She had applied the merest touch of make-up to skin already golden from days in the sun; to eyes made startlingly large with a touch of shadow and a whisper of mascara; to a full mouth that now smiled with a lip-gloss echoing the vivid pink in the print of her full-skirted sundress, its fitted bodice crossing her back in a pair of lattice straps. She had tied her hair back with a scarf and a white linen blazer hung from one hand.

His expression was quickly cloaked. 'You barely made it,' he said, without comment on her appearance.

But she didn't need the words. She had seen his eyes. And, as they made their way down to the jetty, she remembered the shocking kiss that neither of them had wanted. . .and that neither of them had been quite able to resist.

Chay jumped down into the boat, then turned to lift her in, holding her for a moment, suspended in his arms. Sophie, already vulnerable to this man's deadly attraction, felt her lips soften and part under the strong tug of desire. He must know, must feel the wild beating of her pulse as he held her.

The temptation to melt into his arms and take him with her was almost unbearable. Then Nigel's smug smile intervened. This was what he wanted. And afterwards he would want chapter and verse. She pushed herself away and stepped back, breathing a little heavily but infinitely safter on her own feet. 'I think I'll stay out here for a while,' she said quickly.

'It'll be chilly once we're moving,' he objected abruptly, and, taking her arm, led the way to the wheelhouse.

They covered the distance to Sliema at a seemingly breathless rate of knots, while Chay explained the radar and the radio with a briskness that she could not help but envy. Her own feelings were much harder to control. Perched on a high stool beside him, she found her eyes constantly wandering from the instruments to dwell instead on the strong line of his jaw, the passionate curve of his mouth.

He had kissed her. Thrilled her. But she suspected that those angry kisses were simply a foretaste of the pleasure that he might bestow in return for total surrender. He turned and caught her look.

'You're not paying attention,' he said, a little fiercely.

'I. . .I'm sorry.'

'Not half as sorry as you're going to be if you keep looking at me like that.'

'Chay,' she begged, her eyes wide.

'Sophie.' He mimicked her cruelly.

She shot out of her seat to drag in great lungfuls of fresh air, and by the time he had slipped the boat into its berth she was feeling steadier. But he wasn't about to let the matter drop.

'Do you want to tell me about it?' he demanded, as they made their way along the decking to the shore, passing row upon row of expensive and beautiful yachts and powerboats.

'I don't understand.'

'Yes, you do. You're not a child. You're flashing out unmistakable signals. Good God, I could have undressed you on the beach this afternoon and you wouldn't have cared if the Royal Marine Band had been playing a tune while I did it.'

Colour stained her cheeks, but, unable to deny it, she kept her eyes fixed ahead of her, unable to meet his, although she knew he was looking at her with a slightly perplexed expression.

'I don't mean to be a tease. Truly.' Her colour deepened. 'I'm not normally quite so. . .excitable. I'm afraid it's you, Chay.' It was a painful admission.

They had reached his car. He said nothing while he unlocked it and helped her in. But his fingers didn't linger on her arm. The sun had gone and it would soon be dark, but it was stifling inside the car. He lowered the windows then turned to her.

'But?' He refused to let it drop. 'With you there always seems to be a "but".'

'Of course there's a "but". Do you expect me to fall into your bed?'

'Have I asked you to?' His jaw tightened convulsively, and she shook her head. 'But you wish I would?'

Was it that simple for him? 'Wouldn't Poppy object?'

'Poppy?'

'It was three o'clock when you came home last night.'

'Was it?' His eyes gleamed dangerously in the near darkness.

'Well, you hadn't been to bed. . .'

'No,' he agreed. 'I hadn't.' He reached forward and started the engine, reversing the sleek dark shape of the Lotus Esprit out of its parking space and heading towards the town, where the shops had opened for the evening and the streets were filling with people out to enjoy a walk along the promenade.

'Chay,' she said suddenly, relieved to have something, anything, to break the awkward silence. 'Can you take me to a toyshop?'

He threw her an exasperated glance. 'A toyshop?'

'I'd like to get Tom a present for his birthday.'

'You don't have to——'

'I would like to.' Then she bit her lip. 'But. . .'

'But?' he repeated, dangerously.

'I'm afraid you'll have to lend me the money, until you give me back my bag.'

His face darkened, but he executed a sharp turn and drove up into the town, braking sharply in front of a store. It didn't take long to find exactly what she was looking for. A pair of cap-firing six-guns in a holster.

'What do you think?' she asked.

'I think. . .that he'll love them.' He looked around. 'Theresa left some money for Tom to choose something for himself, but I think I'll get that stetson to go with the guns.'

'What have you bought him?' she asked.

'He needed new tack for Melly.'

'Oh,' she said, as she waited for him to pay for her purchases.

'Oh, what?' he demanded, then followed her eye and saw the cowboy outfit hanging on a stand. 'You think he should have something to unwrap on the big day?' She didn't answer. 'We'll take that, too,' he told the assistant.

'Thank you,' she said, as he stowed the packages in the car.

He looked up and met her eyes across the roof of the car. 'Well, now that my son is about to achieve his wildest dreams, do you think we could do something about mine?' He smiled slightly as a slow flush crept across Sophie's cheeks. 'I was actually thinking about dinner,' he murmured.

Overcome by confusion, she ducked into the car. 'Where are we going?'

'The Barracuda, at St Julian's Bay.'

'Oh, yes, I know it.

'Have you been there?' She shook her head; she hadn't, although she had passed the spot frequently. The bay was always full of *dghajsa*, the colourful boats painted with the eye of Osiris to ward off the evil eye, but now the sea was dark, only visible because of the reflection of lights from the buildings that piled almost on top of one another at the water's edge.

They parked a little way from the restaurant, and when Chay took her hand to help her out of the car he did not surrender it, but kept it tucked in his, and Sophie didn't dare pull away.

The restaurant was perched precariously on a sharp bend, hanging out over the harbour with steps that led directly down into the sea like a smuggler's haunt. 'This is lovely,' Sophie exclaimed as she took in the warm, intimate atmosphere, the only lighting the glow from candles at the small tables.

'Two martinis please, George, and a table looking out over the harbour.'

George swept them to a table by the window, quickly whisking away the 'Reserved' sign and placing it on another near by. He brought their drinks and a menu, and lingered to discuss the choice of food and wine with Chay. Sophie sipped her drink and stared out at the lights of the shipping on the horizon, leaving Chay to choose for her. 'You're not allergic to seafood are you, Sophie?' he asked. She shook her head and he ordered for them both.

She felt odd. Light-headed. Maybe it was too much sun, but she didn't think so. She felt drawn by his eyes upon her and turned to face him. Her heart turned over, like a puppy rolling on to its back to have its tummy tickled. No, it definitely wasn't too much sun.

'Tell me about your family,' he said, twisting his glass between his long fingers. 'You've told me about Jennie, but what about your parents?'

'My father is an art teacher at a comprehensive school a few miles from our home, my mother works part-time as a secretary. We're very ordinary people.'

'No boyfriend?'

'No one special.'

'No?' There was an edge to his voice. 'What about the journalist you wanted the photograph for? I thought you said that he was "very special".'

She recalled her angry declaration that first night of her captivity. 'Nigel is. . .' Quite suddenly she wanted to spill out the whole truth. Unburden herself. But if she told him what had really happened when Nigel came to the tower he would never believe that she wasn't up to her eyes in something too nasty for words, and she wouldn't blame him. 'I can't explain.'

'You don't have to explain anything to me, Sophie. I'm the last person to pry into someone else's business,' he said. But she could almost hear the shutters slamming down.

'No. . .' she protested, but he had already turned away from her as George arrived with dishes piled with huge prawns sautéed in their shells.

And what was the point of protesting that he had misunderstood? She could never tell him. She took a large gulp of her martini. It bit like fire at the back of her throat and she gasped. By the time she had recovered the prawns had been served, and she was able to devote her full attention to the task of dismembering them. Perhaps, after all, it was better if he thought she had someone else. Safer.

'The prawns are delicious,' she said at last, in an attempt to break the uncomfortable silence.

'Have you finished?'

She glanced at her plate, surprised to find a pile of debris. She had hardly noticed that she was eating. 'Yes, thank you.'

His glance brought George to clear away. 'So,' he said briskly. 'You'd better tell me what's happening tomorrow.'

And they spent the rest of the meal discussing the arrangements for Tom's beanfeast.

It was odd, she thought, as they drove home in silence, the haunting strains of Sinatra in September mood filling the gap in the conversation, but when Chay had withdrawn from her, the uncomfortable need he had woken in her had seemed to fade. She risked a sideways glance at the hard profile, dark against the dim lights from the dashboard. Could it be that it wasn't just her? That the charge of desire was a two-way circuit and, when he had misunderstood about Nigel, he had somehow broken the connection? It was all very confusing.

He drew up outside the tower and opened the door for her. 'I'll go and put the car away.'

'Do you want coffee?' she asked.

He shook his head. 'No, thanks.' His voice did not encourage her to linger.

'Then I'll see you in the morning.'

But she was in no hurry for bed. Despite her long day she knew she wouldn't sleep. She was still sitting at her dressing-table, brushing her hair, when there was a light tap at the door.

'Sophie?' Chay's voice was muffled through the heavy timber.

'Hold on,' she called, and flew to wrap herself in her flimsy gown before turning the key in the lock and opening the door.

'Was that to keep me out, or you in?' he asked. She didn't answer. She didn't know what had prompted her to turn the key in the lock.

'What do you want?' she demanded.

He thrust her camera bag at her. 'I want you to go. Now.'

'Go?' She stared uncomprehendingly at the bag, then raised her eyes to his. 'That's it?'

'Isn't that enough?'

'No. It's not nearly enough. You keep me here for days against my will, then choose to throw me out in the middle of the night without so much as an apology?'

His eyes darkened slightly, he took a step forward and a frisson of excitment bubbled in her blood. 'An apology?' he demanded. 'What, precisely, should I apologise for?'

Her pulse picked up a beat. This was better. For the last two hours, while he had been polite but withdrawn, she had felt as flat as punched dough. Now suddenly she felt alive again. 'Give me half an hour and I'll write a list,' she offered.

'Don't bother.'

'I won't!'

For a moment they stood facing each other a little breathlessly. 'You'd better pack your things and go before I change my mind.' He turned and began to walk away.

'Right now?' she enquired disbelievingly.

He was back at her side in a single stride, her arm firmly grasped in his hand. 'Damn you, Sophie, but you play dangerous games.'

For a moment she stared at his hand, then quite deliberately raised her eyes to hold his glance. 'Do I?' The question was rhetorical. She knew she was playing with fire, but she couldn't help herself. 'I'm glad to have my freedom, Chay, but it's a little late to do anything about it right now.'

'There are plenty of hotels.'

'Dozens! I should know! But if you want me to leave right this minute, I have to tell you that you still have my suitcase under lock and key!'

An explosive rush of air expelled between his teeth was a warning that she had gone too far. 'Then let's get it. I wouldn't want anything to keep you.' He caught her hand and hauled her after him, up the stairs to the second floor. He reached up and took the key from above the ledge.

'That's what happened to the key,' she said, the words startled from her.

'You didn't expect me to leave it about after you admitted snooping?'

'That was the first place I looked,' she said furiously, then stepped over the threshold. Unlike the floor below there were no dividing walls. It was just one massive room. An artist's studio. Sleeping and work-space in one. Left just as it had been the last time it had been used, a half finished canvas was still propped against an easel. A portrait of a girl. Brushes and paints were heaped anyhow on a work-table. 'This was Matt's room,' she said.

She picked up the photographs of Maria from among the debris. It was the one that had been in Chay's desk.

'The door is locked to keep Tom out. He broke the glass in that photograph and cut himself a few months ago.'

'I see.' She replaced the frame very carefully. 'Will you ever tell him?'

His eyes narrowed, dangerously. 'Tell him?'

She lifted her chin very slightly. 'Will you ever tell Tom that Matt is his father?'

'It was this morning, wasn't it?' he said slowly. 'When we were out riding? I saw something in your face and I had an idea then that I'd said too much.'

'It took me a while to figure it out, Chay, but the dates didn't add up. You didn't arrive in Malta until late in October. Tom was born in April.'

'He could have been premature.'

'You buried your brother, comforted your mother, rushed back, wooed and won Maria and produced a son all within seven months? I said you were fast, Chay. But even you would be hard-pressed to achieve that schedule.'

'Haven't you overlooked the fact that Maria might already have been part of my life?'

'Have I?' she asked. 'I don't think so. You had been away from the island for four years.' Her eyes returned to the photograph of Maria. She could hardly have been more than eighteen or nineteen years old. 'I think Maria would still have been in school then.'

'Did I really tell you all that?' Sophie didn't answer. She didn't really think he wanted her to.

'I wouldn't ever betray you, Chay.' She glanced at him. 'I don't suppose you have any reason to believe that. But it's true, none the less.'

'I don't think you would do anything to hurt Tom,' he said carefully.

'I wouldn't do anything to hurt either of you,' she said, without hesitation. And then with a jolt realised that she meant exactly that. No matter what it cost her.

For a moment he stared at her, then nodded, as if accepting that she meant it. 'You know so much, you might as well know it all.' He swept a pile of papers from a sofa to make room for them both. 'I suppose I should have the lot cleared out,' he said, looking around.

'I do understand.' Her mother had kept Jennie's room as a shrine. 'But from what you've told me about Matt, I think he would find it rather. . .'

'Silly?' he provided, as she struggled for some word that wouldn't offend. 'You're right, of course. He'd laugh his boots off that anyone should take him so seriously.' He lowered himself beside her. 'He never took anything that seriously.'

'Not even Maria?' she asked. 'She was the secret, wasn't she?'

'You remember everything, don't you?'

'Everything.' Everything connected with Chay Buchanan. She thought she would remember this week for the rest of her life in brilliant rainbow-bright detail.

'After the funeral I came back here to clear up the loose ends. I intended to sell the lease on the tower, try and forget what had happened. But the day I came back Maria arrived, distraught, on the doorstep. It took a long time to get the whole story from her.'

Sophie remembered his interest in Jennie and began to understand a little. 'Had her family turned her out?'

'Oh, no. Quite the reverse. She had escaped—climbed down a drainpipe, apparently.' He smiled slightly. 'She must have had considerable practice during her assignations with Matt, since she was already betrothed to a man her family had carefully chosen for her. They are old people. A noble family, from the Mdina.' Then his face grew grim again. 'They had only one answer for the sort of disgrace she had brought to them. She had been told she would be kept out of sight until her baby was delivered and then she would be sent away, to the convent.'

'I've seen it. At least the outside.' Grim walls, bars. The guide had told her that the only way out for the nuns was in a coffin. And that was a concession only granted as recently as twenty years ago. Before that the nuns had even been buried in a cemetery within the convent grounds. She shuddered. 'So you let her stay.'

'Yes, I let her stay. But that wasn't enough. Maria thought it would be, that I could protect her. It wasn't that simple. And her brothers were at the door within the hour, demanding that I hand her over.' He laid a finger along his nose. 'A memorable encounter.' He shrugged awkwardly. 'I told them the child she was carrying was mine and that we were going to be married. I don't think they believed me, but they gave me a week. If we weren't married by then, they would be back.'

'Not long.'

'No, but I didn't need to be pushed. I was afraid they might still return mob-handed in the night to try to reclaim her, and without a passport I couldn't even get her out of the country. So we were married within three days by the British High Commissioner. It was the only way I could be certain that Matt's child wouldn't just disappear to be adopted by some unknown family.' He sat forward, staring at his hands. 'He was a Buchanan, entitled to everything that Matt had, that I could give him. When Tom was born it was like getting a small piece of my brother returned to me.' He looked at her then. 'A kind of forgiveness.'

CHAPTER NINE

'You didn't tell anyone?'

Chay shook his head. 'My mother had to know. But Maria's family had sufficient influence to keep any mention of the family name out of the newspapers, so it wasn't picked up by the British nationals. You do see? I couldn't take the risk that they would take Tom. But once my name was on the birth certificate, he was mine——'

'Yes, I understand.' She covered his hand with her own. 'Truly.' But her heart bled too for Maria, a young girl who had married a stranger to protect her child.

'Why did you stay here afterwards?' she asked. 'I would have thought——'

'Don't you think I wanted to go?' he turned on her angrily. 'I never wanted to set foot in this place again. It was Maria. She refused to leave. She stayed up here in Matt's room day and night. . . I should have known then that it could only end in disaster. But I threw myself into research for my next book and hoped that once the child was born she would snap out of it.

'Just after Tom was born I had to go to London for the launch of a book I had finished the year before. The publishers had arranged the usual round of chat-shows and interviews, and to tell the truth I was the last person in the world Maria wanted about her. Matt and I weren't twins, like you and Jennie, but we were very alike. She must have found it hard to take. I hoped that, if I left, she might begin to recover her spirits, take some interest in the baby.' He let out a low, soft breath. 'Theresa had come a few months before Tom was born—she had looked after Maria as a child—and Paul promised to keep an eye on her. . . I thought she would be all right.'

'Paul knows?'

'It's a little difficult to keep something like that from a doctor. And he knew Matt.'

'What happened, Chay?'

He sat back and stared up at the ceiling. 'Publicity happened.' He closed his eyes. 'I hadn't told Poppy that I had married. I didn't quite trust her not to use wedding-bells for a little extra hype, and I wasn't in a position to produce the blushing bride for the obligatory photographs. In the event, of course, I was presented as the literary world's eligible bachelor, a girl thrust on my arm whenever there was a camera pointed in my direction. Maria must have seen the photographs in the papers. Her family certainly had.'

'But surely Paul——'

'If Paul had known what was happening he might have been able to help. But Gian's mother had been taken desperately ill and they had rushed off to Florence to be with her.' He paused painfully. 'Maria swallowed a handful of paracetamol. She didn't mean to kill herself. . .it was a cry for help. But no one heard.'

'Oh, Chay. How pitiful.'

'It was a couple of days before Theresa realised there was something wrong. The symptoms take longer than sleeping pills but are just as deadly. I flew straight back, but by then it was already too late to do much more than pray. She made me promise to stay at the tower, Matt's home. She wanted Tom to know he was Maltese, to learn to speak her language. And she wanted me to try and reconcile her family to the boy. . .' His voice cracked on the words, and as he turned to her she took him in her arms and held him, her own cheeks wet against his shirt-front.

It was a long time before he held her away from him. 'Sophie——'

'It's all right, Chay. No matter what happens, I'll never betray your trust. Never.' She held his head between her hands. 'Believe me.'

His eyes held hers. 'That was the reason I couldn't let you go. Maria's family pride was frozen stiff with the disgrace. And how they hated me staying here. They wanted the whole thing swept under the carpet. They even sent a lawyer, threatening all kinds of problems if I didn't take the boy and leave the island.'

'Dear God. What did they do?'

'Nothing I couldn't handle.' But his face tightened at the memory. 'He was their grandchild, and for Maria I was determined they would never be allowed to ignore him or forget him. I took him to the cathedral every Sunday because I knew they would be there. And I knew, that first day, when Maria's mother saw him, that I had one friend. Theresa brought a letter from her. Be patient, she said. Be quiet. And I have been very quiet. Nothing to cause a ripple of publicity of any kind.'

'So you stopped writing and became a respectable businessman instead.'

'I tried to stop writing. I quickly realised that was impossible, but I told Poppy that I had burned myself out. The bills didn't stop coming in, though. I was halfway to qualifying as an architect when my first book was published. The tourist industry was booming, so property development seemed the obvious choice. And every time Maria's father saw my logo it served as a reminder that I wasn't going to go away.'

'He's had plenty to remind him. I've seen your boards everywhere.'

'Have you?' His look was long, assessing.

'I found a business card. . . When Poppy mentioned your business. . .'

'It hardly matters. You know everything else.'

'Not quite. What is going to happen on Sunday? You said it wouldn't matter after Sunday.'

'Maria's father has finally relented. A heart-attack has apparently given him a glimpse of his own mortality. On Sunday, Sophie, after the most delicate negotiations with his lawyers, Maria's father is going to receive his grandson.' He raised one shoulder slightly. 'You came blundering into that, threatening all kinds of mayhem. I couldn't take the risk.'

There had never been any risk. But it hardly seemed to matter now. 'You've sacrificed so much——'

'No. I gave Maria my promise. I would do it twice over if necessary.'

'Thank you for telling me. Your trust. . .is a precious gift.' Sophie reached up and kissed him lightly on the mouth. For a moment nothing happened. Then with a groan he gathered her into his arms and he kissed her. There was nothing of the practised flirt or the arrogant predator about his embrace. It was simply a man holding a woman, kissing her because that was what he wanted to do more than anything else in the world. And Sophie responded unreservedly, with a delight that shimmered through her.

'Sophie. . .' he murmured. His breath was soft on her eyelashes and her arms curled about his neck like a silk scarf and drew him down to her. For one hectic, rollercoaster moment, as he kissed her with a fierce, almost angry intensity, she thought she would die of happiness.

Then without warning he broke away, and, ignoring her soft cry of loss, held her at arm's length, as if she represented some mortal danger. And, as he stared at her, it seemed to Sophie that her fate hung in the balance.

He stood up and turned away. 'Go to bed, Sophie. Now.'

'Chay. . .?' Her voice quivered with the shock of his rejection. They had been on the edge of something so beautiful, so thrilling. . .his dismissal was like a blow. But his back remained turned resolutely towards her and after a moment she turned and stumbled down the stairs.

Sophie was about to start Tom's birthday cake when the doorbell rang the following morning.

'Sophie,' Poppy smiled, swept into the hall without waiting to be invited, and stepped past her.

'Chay's out,' Sophie informed the woman's back. When she had crawled miserably from her bed that morning, just after dawn, there had been no sign of him.

There was the minutest pause. 'Mmm. I know.' Poppy turned with a delicately teasing laugh that must have taken hours of practice to perfect and quite set Sophie's teeth on edge. 'I've. . .er. . .just left him,' she said, managing to load the words with hidden meaning. A burning blush betrayed Sophie. It was barely eight o'clock. Chay hadn't left very early this morning. He had left very late last night. 'I've called to collect his manuscript.' She regarded Sophie with a touch of amusement. 'He told me where it is,' she said. 'Don't let me keep you from your chores.'

Sophie turned on her heel. It was none of her business, she reminded herself as she returned to the kitchen, what Chay got up to with Poppy, or if he had decided to go ahead with publication of his book now that everything was going to be settled with Tom's grandfather. Although after waiting so long it seemed a little careless. . .

But last night she had been so sure that *she* was the one he had wanted to hold in his arms. . . She cracked the eggs into a bowl and began to beat them ferociously, not sure whether it was Chay or Poppy she wanted to reduce to batter.

She jumped a little while later, as the door banged after Poppy, then sagged against the work-top, unable to support herself any longer, and let the bitter tears fall.

Half an hour later she had pulled herself together and was beating sugar and butter to cream when she sensed Chay's presence. The mixer had drowned out the noise of his arrival. And even as she refused to acknowledge him he leaned over her shoulder and hooked his finger through the mixture. 'Mmm, chocolate.'

'Don't do that,' she warned tetchily.

'Or?'

She turned and looked up over her shoulder. 'Or I shall have to slap your wrist,' she threatened, a little shaken by the unexpected closeness of a mouth bracketed by the deeply carved lines of a smile. He must have been home for a while because he had showered, and moisture still clung to the thick mop of dark hair. And, having finally gained her full attention, he dropped a kiss tasting of cake mixture on her mouth.

'Why don't you try? he invited. Her heart gave a painful little gasp and, apparently satisfied, he moved to the table and picked up a list. 'Are you in a desperate hurry for any of this, because I'll be a while?'

And she could imagine just what would take the time. 'Don't rush back,' she advised coldly. 'But, if you can *spare the time*, there is something you can do for me.'

'Oh? What's that?' His voice had lost some of its warmth, the message was getting through.

She kept her eyes on the mixture she was beating. 'Book me a flight home for Sunday. As early in the day as possible.' She couldn't stand the long, empty silence that folllowed this request. 'I have to deliver the photographs to Island Holidays at the beginning of the week,' she rushed on. 'And then I have a job booked in—'

'Liverpool. You said. You're not the only one with a retentive memory.' She turned, pleading silently for him to understand, but his eyes had shut her out. 'And I imagine that you can't wait to get home and file your story. It must merit quite a bonus.'

Wrong. The bonus was to have been for something else entirely. 'I'm not a journalist,' she said flatly.

'But your "very special" friend Nigel is.'

I won't tell him! Never! But the words remained locked in her head, and she was still rooted furiously to the spot when the front door banged shut behind him. It didn't matter, she told herself. Eventually he would know that she hadn't betrayed him.

So what? that cruel inner voice taunted her. Last night had meant nothing. He had held her close and kissed her simply because she had been there, to listen while he poured out his grief and guilt; if he had swept her into his bed it might just have been perfect. But he had gone to Poppy instead, and any delay in leaving would simply prolong the agony.

And on Sunday evening Nigel would be coming for his pound of flesh. She was determined to be gone long before then.

Chay returned early in the afternoon and dumped the shopping on the kitchen table, along with the flight confirmation and a courier bag with her films. He curtly declined her offer of a late lunch and departed for the beach with Twany to begin building the barbeque. The fact that he had apparently got the message did little to restore her spirits.

He returned late in the afternoon, took a beer from the fridge and offered her one. She took it gratefully. She normally hated drinking anything from a can, but Chay had simply ripped the ring-pull off his and tipped it up, to drink long and deep, and she followed suit, too hot from a day spent over a cooker to care about such niceties.

'Have you checked your films?' he asked, leaning back against the table.

'They'll wait until I get home. I'll need my light-box to choose the best. I suppose you've taken out. . .?'

'I've taken out the personal ones. They're very good.'

'Consider them a contribution to your family album,' she snapped, and his face darkened. 'I'm sorry,' she said, quickly. 'After what you told me last night. . . that was tactless.'

'After last night I thought we were well beyond the point where the word tact would have a place in our relationship.' He threw the can in the bin. 'I clearly misread the signals.' He turned, the muscles in his neck corded with tension. 'Or did you spend the long night hours dreaming about Nigel? Or perhaps the handsome Cesare?'

'No!'

'Then doubtless you've had time to do your sums and realise how much your story is worth.' She was too angry to answer. 'You'd better go and get ready,' he said abruptly. 'We're due at Gian and Paul's in half an hour.'

She stiffened. 'I think I'd prefer to stay here.'

'Then think again, lady. They're expecting you.'

She fought back the urge to defy him. He looked fit to drag her there. 'If you insist.'

'In this particular case, I'm afraid I do.'

'Meaning?' she demanded, and regretted it the moment the word was out of her mouth.

He lunged forward and seized her arm. 'Meaning, Sophie Nash, that the next time you flash "come to bed" out of those big grey eyes of yours, don't expect me to act the gentleman if you should change your mind at the last minute.'

'Gentleman!' She almost exploded.

'Good God, do you think it was easy to send you away last night?' His fingers were biting into her arm as he held her pinned against him. Her breathing was ragged and she was held by a pair of eyes that generated enough electricity to power the national grid. 'But you are a very unwilling guest in my house, Sophie. Taking you to my bed would have been in the worst possible taste, don't you think?'

She knew that he was a hair's breadth from kissing her, and she mustn't allow that to happen. Ever again. She wrenched herself free. 'Especially when there's a more than willing reserve!'

'What the hell is that supposed to mean?' His dark brows drew together.

'Oh, don't be bashful, Chay. When Poppy dropped by she certainly wasn't——'

'Poppy was here?'

'She came to pick up your manuscript.'

'So. That was——' He broke off. 'Did you see her take anything?'

'No. I didn't stick around. I don't find her company that appealing.'

He pushed her through to the study and swung back a large painting to reveal a safe. Her searching had been pointless. She hadn't even thought of a safe. 'There!' He threw the pile of notepads on to the desk.

'I don't understand.'

'Poppy, thanks to you, is convinced I have a book just waiting to be published. In fact there are three. A trilogy. But even you didn't know that. So this morning I had a message from her husband, saying he was interested in leasing a berth at the new marina and could he meet me there. And while I was conveniently out of the way Poppy called, hoping to find a manuscript. But she could hardly expect you to stand by while she ransacked the study. So she made sure you wouldn't hang around. The only way she was certain would work.'

Poppy was married? 'She didn't——'

'No. She didn't get anything. No thanks to you.'

'I'm sorry.'

'Go and change, Sophie. We're going to be late as it is.'

In normal circumstances it would have been a delightful evening. Paul and Gian were welcoming; Cesare was on his best behaviour. His light-hearted charm was a million miles away from Chay's withdrawn, slightly dark mood and when he held out a glass of wine and raised his brows at the vacant chair beside her, Sophie's smile was welcoming.

He had clearly come to the conclusion that she and Chay had had a row and set out to amuse her, telling her about his job as a pilot with a commercial airline.

'I come to London sometimes,' he told her. 'May I call you?'

She hesitated. He was a pleasant companion, but without the glowering presence of Chay to restrain his ardour. . . 'I have some pretty friends,' she countered. 'I'm sure they'd love to meet you.'

'Give me your number quickly, *cara*. . .' he said with a soft laugh.

'She's not on the telephone.' Chay took Sophie's arm and jerked her to her feet. 'It's time to go. Tom's nearly out on his feet.'

And it was only Tom's presence in the car that prevented her from telling him exactly what she thought of him. The child curled up in her lap and by the time they were home was fast asleep. Chay took him from her and carried him off to bed, curtly declining any help.

Feeling slightly lost, she gathered up her films and went upstairs, thinking that she might begin to pack. But she didn't have her suitcase, and by the time she fetched it from upstairs she was too tired to do anything other than fall into bed.

Gian and Paul were the first to arrive with their brood the following afternoon and Paul immediately departed for the beach to help Chay. After that the children arrived thick and fast. Gian looked over their heads. 'How many did you say there are supposed to be? We'd better keep count in case we lose one or two.'

'Sixteen from school, your three and Tom. Twenty.' They had a quick count-up and led them down to the beach.

All the children had made an effort to come as cowboys and cowgirls and even some of the girls had guns. Led by Tom, they fired their caps off furiously, until the sound ricocheted around the cliff and the air was filled with the sharp scent of the explosive. For ten minutes they were allowed to let off steam in a gunfight that would have done justice to the OK Corral. Then Sophie began to organise games while Chay and Paul started the barbecue.

At about four the men began to cook, while Sophie

and Gian took the children into the sea to cool off. It seemed forever before Chay banged on a tin plate with a huge wooden spoon and they could hand them over to be fed. Sophie sank gratefully on to the sand and closed her eyes for a few minutes.

Despite a series of disturbed nights, sleep had eluded her as she had tried to order her thoughts through the long night. It had almost been a relief to get up as the dawn broke to ice Tom's cake.

Breakfast had been all excitement, with Tom opening his presents, then Chay had taken him down to the stables to get him out from under her feet. There had barely been time for a quick lunch before Gian and Paul had arrived. But at least there hadn't been time for any awkward silences.

'I hope you're not asleep.' Chay's voice seemed to come from a long way off, but she lifted a hand in a half-hearted way. She wasn't asleep, she wanted to say, but it was too much effort. 'You do know how dangerous it is to fall asleep in the sun?' he persisted. Why wouldn't he go away? 'Sophie?' She forced one eye open to convince him and was just in time to see the water coming, but far too late to avoid it. It hit her, icy cold, in the stomach, and she came up with a yell. 'I'm so glad that you're not asleep.'

He had been in the sea, presumably to cool off after the cooking, and water was running down the broad expanse of his chest, dripping from the tousled mop of dark hair, and somewhere in the ocean depths of his eyes, he was laughing.

Sophie saw a dangerous shade of red that brought her up from the sand in one fluid movement, and she flung herself at him. He stood his ground for a second, as if transfixed, then he turned and ran, urged on by the delighted children.

His long legs quickly out-distanced her but she

pounded after him in mindless determination, following him behind a group of rocks that took them out of sight of the party. Then she stopped. He had disappeared. There was a small cave that had been gouged from the cliff-wall by the constant wearing motion of the sea and she stepped towards it.

'Chay?' she called uncertainly. Then she shrieked as he grabbed her from behind and pushed her into the cave. 'Let go of me!' she demanded as he turned her, caught her with one arm about the waist and held her fast.

'But you've caught me,' he protested, without much regard for the truth. 'The question is, Miss Sophie Nash, what are you going to do with me?'

'Nothing! Let me go, Chay. I'm soaked!'

'So you are.' A wicked smile lifted the corners of his mouth as he regarded the T-shirt, thrown over her swimsuit to protect her skin, which now clung wetly to her body, offering no hiding place for embarrassingly prominent nipples that seemed to peak in almost automatic response to his merest touch. Now, inches from his bronzed torso clad only in his tormentingly brief swimsuit, her body almost groaned with longing for him. As if he heard, he tightened his grip, drawing her closer, so that the rough hair on his legs grazed her soft thighs, her tell-tale breasts were pressed against his chest, and her abdomen. . . She gasped as she realised just what was pressed against her abdomen, the shock bringing some semblance of control to her disordered senses.

'Chay. . .the children. . .'

'The children are occupied. However, I could be persuaded, for the payment of a small forfeit—a kiss, I believe, is traditional. . .?'

It wasn't fair. He shouldn't do this to her. She wanted to be strong, but held like this, pressed against the unyielding strength of his body, escape was the last thing on her mind. And his eyes, more blue than green, as if reflecting the flawless sky, told her that he knew exactly what she wanted. 'I thought I had captured you. . .'

'Possession, Sophie, is nine-tenths of the law,' he reminded her, and her lips parted on a little breath of excitement, her lids fluttering down as his mouth descended with agonising slowness. His lips touched the delicate hollow of her cheek, sending a delicious tingle rippling through her skin to every part of her body, and for a moment she remained perfectly still, waiting, knowing that this was just a prelude. . . To nothing. She opened her eyes.

'You've had your forfeit, Sophie. Don't be greedy.' He turned her round and gave her a little push. 'Hadn't you better go back and give Gian a hand?'

Tom hurtled up to her as she stumbled back along the beach to rejoin the others. 'Are we going to have the cake now?' he asked.

'Not on the beach. You can blow out your candles and cut the cake when everyone comes later to collect your friends. Have you all had enough to eat?'

'Sure thing!'

Sophie managed a convincing smile at his attempt at a cowboy accent. 'Well, then, we'd better get on with the sandcastle competition, pardner,' she said, diverting her eyes firmly away from the spot where Chay was tugging on a pair of shorts.

She organised everyone with spades and set them to work. Gian smiled as she dropped down beside her.

'Well? Did you give that naughty boy what he deserved?' she asked.

'What? Oh, Chay. Sure, I beat him to a pulp,' she said, imitating Tom.

'Is that what they're calling it now?' Sophie looked

up sharply, but it was nothing but the mildest teasing. She sighed. She was the one who felt she had been pulped.

'That was the most exhausting afternoon I have ever spent.' Chay closed the door behind the last of their guests. After a spectacular firework display, made especially by Twany for Tom's birthday, Tom had cut his cake and handed it round to the children while Chay and Sophie had offered something more substantial to their parents.

Now he put his hands on her shoulders and looked down into her face. 'Thank you for today, Sophie. Tom had a great time.' He smiled. 'I rather think I did too.'

She had made a point of keeping her distance from him since he had made a fool of her on the beach. Now he was too close, and she was much too vulnerable. 'Where is Tom?' she asked rather briskly, moving away.

He dropped his hands and looked around. 'He was here a minute ago.' They found him asleep on the sofa in front of the fireplace, his gun still clutched in a grubby hand. Chay stood over him for a moment. 'I'll take him up to bed. Why don't you make us both a drink?' he said, scooping up the sleeping child.

She poured him a Scotch and herself a glass of wine, then fetched a tray and began to gather up the glasses and plates. She was carrying it through to the kitchen when Chay came down the stairs.

'Did he wake up?'

'No. I took off most of his things and tucked him in. I'm afraid he's rather grubby and he hasn't brushed his teeth.'

'I don't suppose they will drop out overnight. Can you open this door, please? Your drink is in the drawing-room.'

'I'll fetch it and come and give you a hand.'

'There's no need.' She was tetchy. He was too masculine, too desirable. She wanted him too much, and since she couldn't have him, she didn't want him near her. Not if he was going to tease her, poke fun at the desire he knew tormented her, as he had done on the beach.

'I'll be the judge of that.' He took the tray from her and put it on the draining-board. 'This is my house, Sophie, even though you seem to have turned it on its head from the moment you arrived.'

'You made me stay,' she reminded him, a stubborn tilt to her chin as she turned on the taps and let hot water run into the sink.

'Well, you have your flight booked tomorrow. There's apparently nothing more to keep you.'

'Great.' She dumped a pile of plates in the sink and began to wash them, heaping them on the draining-board with a noisy clatter.

Chay began to dry them and stack them neatly. 'You will take a little more care with the glasses, won't you?' he asked, as she reached for a crystal tumbler. She swished it around the suds with restrained violence and set it to drain with excessive care. As she reached for the next he caught her wrist. 'I couldn't care less about the glasses, Sophie, but wouldn't want you to cut yourself.' Tears sprang unbidden to her eyes and she bit her lip, trying desperately not to let them fall. 'Sophie?'

She blinked furiously. 'Yes?' she croaked, her throat tight, her voice hoarse.

'What is it?' He turned her to face him, but she refused to look up. 'What's the matter? You're like a prickly pear this evening.'

'Green and spiky,' she hiccuped as she blinked back the tears and faced him. 'Well, thanks.'

'Just spiky.' He brushed the tears away with his thumbs. 'Is it because I didn't kiss you this afternoon?'

Damn him! Why did he always see straight through her? Worse, why did he have to say it out loud? It was bad enough that he knew, without him insisting she admit it. 'You did kiss me.' She managed a whisper.

'Not quite the way either of us intended. You must surely have realised——?'

'Must I? Why don't you run it by me, Chay?' she invited. All her desires were apparently hanging out for the world and his wife to see. It would adjust the balance, soothe her pride, if instead of that superior know-it-all smirk just this once he had to admit his own arousal. 'Tell me how it was for you.'

His face was gratifyingly grave. 'For me, Sophie? It was like this. If I had kissed you, I don't believe anything could ever have stopped me until I had tasted every last part of you. And then made love to you until we were both exhausted.'

'Oh!' The sound came in a little rush of breath. Whatever she had expected, it hadn't been that.

'Not quite the time or place, was it? Now, shall we finish washing the glasses? Or had you something else in mind?'

'Oh, er, yes. . .the glasses.' She turned back to the sink and stared at the crystal. 'At least. . . I'm sorry. I don't think I can,' she said, as her legs began to tremble.

'You did ask,' he reminded her, and then with a muffled oath he swept her into his arms and carried her into the drawing-room, to the sofa set four-square before the fireplace. 'This is ridiculous, Sophie,' he murmured into her hair.

She didn't want it to be ridiculous. She wanted to bury her face in the warmth of his neck and let him hold her and never let her go. But she resisted the urge, held herself away from him. 'Is it? You were the one who insisted upon playing the gentleman.'

'I had to.'

'Even if it was what I wanted?'

'Even then,' he said.

She took a little heart from the hoarseness of his voice, and peeped up at him from beneath long lashes. 'Maybe I could persuade you to change your mind.' He caught his breath as a delicate flush coloured her cheekbones.

'Sophie. . .' he warned her. 'What on earth am I going to do with you?'

Her blush deepened. 'I was rather hoping you knew, Chay,' she whispered into his neck. 'I've done the theory, but I never could. . .quite get through the practical.'

There was a pause. 'And you carry a packet of condoms with you in case the opportunity. . .er. . . arises to take a re-test?'

CHAPTER TEN

FOR a moment his words didn't quite penetrate the warm, comfortable haze generated by Chay's arms wrapped about her. When it did, when the implication of what he had said finally broke through the rosy glow, cruelly shredding it, Sophie erupted from his arms, and he made no move to hold her.

They had come a long way in a few short days, but this was the most brutal reminder of the true status of their relationship. That when he had first brought her to the tower he had searched her bags to find out who she was, knew things about her that no other man had ever come close to touching. And because of that he thought she was lying to him.

When her shaky legs had put ten feet between them she finally managed to speak. 'I might be a twenty-three-year-old virgin, Chay Buchanan, but that doesn't make me stupid. My sister——' her voice almost cracked with the hurt of his disbelief '—my twin sister, was an unmarried mother by the time she was seventeen. It was like looking into a mirror. . . The resulting mess left a lasting impression on me. I have no intention. . .' She saw the beginning of a smile across his lips. 'It's not funny!' she said angrily.

He was beside her in a stride, his strong arms around her preventing further retreat. 'I agree, my love. It's not in the least bit funny. It's just. . .' He tilted her face up to his, forced her to look at him. 'Tell me, how long have you been carrying that packet about with you?'

'Ever since. . .' She flushed crimson and her hands

flew to her hot cheeks. 'Do you think they've passed their "sell by" date?'

'I really don't think I'd be prepared to risk it,' he said, with the utmost seriousness.

'I. . . I didn't think.'

He finally allowed himself to smile. 'Do you know, Sophie, that is one of the things I most love about you? You just jump in with both feet. I begin to believe that you are congenitally incapable of deception.' He drew her against his chest briefly, and buried his face in her hair.

You'd better tell him, Sophie, her little voice prompted. Right now. But she ignored it. There was plenty of time for explanations. She needed this moment, just to be held by him.

After a while, when she didn't say anything, he held her away from him and looked down into her face. 'Sophie Nash, do you know that you could break a man's heart? Just by looking at him like that?'

'I. . .I would never want to break yours, Chay. I would never want to hurt you in any way.' For a brief dizzy moment he kissed her, then he tore himself away.

'I'll go and open a bottle of champagne,' he said, a little raggedly. 'We've got a few things to discuss.'

'No, don't go. . .' she murmured, reaching for him in a sudden panic at the thought of him leaving her on her own. 'I must tell you. . .'

He drew in a sharp breath. 'If you don't let me go right now, Sophie, I swear you'll suffer the same fate as your sister.'

'I. . .I'm not seventeen any more, Chay.'

He swore softly. 'You're playing with fire, Sophie. I'm not made of wood.'

'Chay. . .' she protested—but to an empty doorway. 'This is ridiculous,' she finished, but talking to herself. But wonderfully ridiculous. She curled up in an armchair and laid her cheek against its broad arm, and hugged the thought to herself.

As she lay against the old worn leather, a bright packet of prints on a low table in the direct line of her sight intruded on her thoughts. They had been brought over by Gian and left for them to look at. She reached almost automatically for it and began to flip through the pictures. Quite ordinary snapshots in the main part, of their day on the beach, until she came to the photograph of Chay and Tom grinning over a bright red apple. She smiled. It was a real winner; she had known it would be the moment she had taken it. Then, as if a goose had walked over her grave, she shivered. If he saw it he would think she had done it deliberately. That she had planned it. . . She pushed it into her shorts-pocket as she heard him coming back.

She turned, forcing a smile to her lips, certain her guilt must be written clear for him to see. Then the photograph was wiped from her mind as she saw the second man, grinning broadly in ghastly contrast to the hard-edged danger of Chay's expression, as they crossed the endless expanse of the room and came towards her. Nigel. For a moment the room swam. It couldn't be him. It was Saturday, she wanted to scream. She had another day before Nigel came to demand her happiness in exchange for Jennie's. Time to explain, time to tell Chay everything. But there was no more time.

She saw the anger glitter in Chay's eyes and knew that nothing she could say would ever put things right. 'You have a visitor, Sophie.' Chay's voice was like a splinter in her heart. 'The cavalry has arrived to rescue you, apparently.' He stared at her as if he was seeing a stranger. 'Just a fraction too soon.'

'I didn't hear the door. . .' she said stupidly.

'That's because your friend was flashing his headlights across the road in the expectation that you would notice him. That was the signal you arranged when he called?' he asked, with deadly scorn.

She leapt to her feet. 'Chay, this isn't. . . I didn't——'

But Nigel interrupted, making a liar of her. 'Sorry if I interrupted something special, sweetheart, but my deadline has been moved up. I couldn't wait until tomorrow.'

'I've nothing for you, Nigel,' she said dully.

'We had a deal. . .' Nigel warned. 'Remember Jennie. . .'

'A deal?' Chay regarded the man with distaste. 'I'm afraid if you want the photographs, they have already been destroyed.'

But Nigel didn't care what Chay thought of him. He was used to people looking at him as if he was something nasty they had trodden in. 'I know,' he said smugly, and ran his hand up her arm. 'She told me when I called.'

'No. . .' Sophie moaned softly at the innuendo he had managed to insinuate into those innocent words.

'But after a few days tucked up with you she guaranteed that she could provide me with something far more interesting.'

Chay's eyes were flint, all the colour gone from them. 'That was your deal? How unfortunate for you both that I didn't seize the many opportunities thrown in my path.' He stared at Sophie. 'Don't be too hard on her. She really did try.' Chay, his face all black and white shadows in the lamplight, took a step towards him. 'But you had better take the. . .lady. . .home now. I'm sure she has more than enough to excite your readers.'

Nigel, edging back towards the door, was no longer smiling quite so confidently.

Sophie swung back to Chay, determined to convince him that this was none of her doing. 'Chay, listen to me. . .'

His eyes were riveted to her face. Leaden eyes, in which contempt for them both was written clear. 'I think,' he said, ignoring her plea, his voice hard and cold as black marble, 'that the sooner you both leave my home, the better.'

'Come on, Sophie,' Nigel coaxed.

'Are you still here?' Chay's eyes finally released her as he made a sudden move in Nigel's direction.

Realising that he was in imminent danger of being pitched bodily through the door, Nigel hastily backed off. 'I'll wait in the car while you get your things,' he threw at Sophie. Then he fled.

She tried to move—to go to Chay, tell him, make him understand that she hadn't wanted to be a part of Nigel's sordid little plot to uncover his secrets. But nothing seemed to work. Her legs, her arms, her tongue were all made of wood. And her brain seized up beneath the glacial expression that forbade any attempt at explanation. Was it only fifteen minutes since he had held her? Kissed her?

'I'm truly sorry that I didn't understand how badly you wanted me to take you to bed, Sophie, to put the final touch to your. . .story.' His voice sliced through her heart like a knife. 'Especially when you offered yourself with such flattering frequency, even to the point of tempting me with the special prize of your virginity. I really must try to be less. . .'

'Noble?' she said quietly.

'Gullible.'

A sob broke from her lips and she turned and ran, passing the abandoned champagne and glasses standing on the hall table, up the stairs to her room. She flung her clothes into the case, bundling them up with no attempt to fold them. He had said she could break his heart. Well, he had just broken hers, not trusting her, not giving her a chance to explain. And why on earth should he believe her? Trust her? She had, after all, been part of a plot. . . But she hadn't realised. . . How could she have known that she would fall in love?

She banged the case shut and took one last look around. It felt like the end of something, but how could that be so? Nothing had started. Only love, and that apparently didn't need time. She fought back the longing to take a last glance at Tom. Instead she walked down the stairs and through the hall, eyes straight ahead, to where Chay was waiting grey-faced at the front door. He caught her arm and she stopped, but refused to look at him. 'Why?' he demanded.

For a moment, for just a moment, she thought she had a chance, that she could explain why. But deep down she knew it wouldn't make any difference. Nothing could. It would simply prolong the agony of parting. 'It was just a job,' she said.

He abruptly released her, and as she stepped through the door and out into the night it was slammed behind her and the lock was turned.

The sound of rain woke her. It was days since she had returned to London. Days in which the rain had sounded a constant background to the ringing of the telephone that she left unanswered. She jumped as it began again, and she glanced at the clock. Seven-thirty. He knew she would be gone by eight. Work. Any sort of work, to keep her mind busy so she wouldn't have to think. She lifted the receiver, cut off the call and left it off the hook, then swung her feet out of bed, shivering in the chill of a spring that in London refused to blossom.

She made tea and poured cereal into a bowl, though

she knew she couldn't eat. The doorbell rang. It would be Sarah from next door, checking up on her. Worrying about her. But it wasn't Sarah, it was Nigel, his foot in the door before she could slam it. He pushed his way in.

'Go away. I have nothing to say to you.'

He took an envelope from his pocket, holding it under her eyes so that she was forced to look at it. 'I went to see Jennie last night,' he said. 'She's got this flu that's going round. Looks pretty poorly. They go through these places like. . . Well, you know. I expect the kid will get it soon.'

'How can you?' she demanded bitterly. 'How can you be so. . .evil?'

'Evil? That's a bit strong, Sophie. All I want in return for her address is everything you know about Chay Buchanan. He said you knew plenty.'

'Nothing that I'm prepared to talk to you about.'

'Pity. Your sister——'

'My sister is a grown woman, Nigel. She can come home any time she wants. It's taken this for me to realise that.' She took a step towards him. 'But the truth is, Nigel, that I don't believe you know where my sister is. I poured my heart out to you because it was my birthday and hers, and I had had a glass too much wine at a party. And miraculously, it seemed, through your contacts, you found her. Just a little *too* miraculously. Because there was just a little favour you wanted for the information. Since I was going to Malta anyway. Something else I had mentioned at the party.' She took another step towards him. 'And I so much wanted to believe you that I would have done anything. You knew that, didn't you? It's the stock-in-trade of people like you.'

His eyes hardened and he gripped the envelope

between his fingers, holding it out as he tore it to shreds. 'You'll never know now, will you?'

The pieces fluttered to the carpet. She knew. Until that moment she hadn't truly been certain. But while there had been a chance he could have used the information he would never have thrown it away.

'You don't understand, do you, Nigel?' She looked him in the face. 'Even if I had believed you, it would have made no difference.' Then she picked up the pieces, all quite blank, walked into the kitchen and dropped them in the bin.

But she had been right, and for a moment a mixture of pain and relief flooded through her, making her weak. She had promised Chay. In the quiet darkness of the tower, when he had told her about Maria and Matt, she had promised that she would never betray him. Even for her sister.

And the agony of letting Jennie go had somehow cleared her mind. The more she thought, the more she had been sure. She wiped away a tear, suddenly feeling a little better. Chay had said, with some justification, that she jumped in with both feet. That was what had got her into this mess in the first place. But not this time. This time she had done the right thing.

She went back into the living-room and looked around, but Nigel had gone. She walked across to the door and closed it behind him, thankful that she need never see or speak to him again.

Sophie walked across to the bedside table to replace the receiver on the telephone and glanced at her clock. There was plenty of time for a shower to wash the stench of the man away. Then she frowned, and knelt on the floor to look beneath the bed in case it had fallen. But it hadn't fallen. It wasn't there. Her beautiful photograph of Chay and Tom. The photograph that she had found in the pocket of her shorts after the nightmare journey home. The photograph that she had stood beside her bed in a little silver frame. It was gone.

Nigel.

She flew to the phone to call the police. The frame was antique. She would have him arrested for theft. Then she stopped. There was no time for that. She had to warn Chay, and there was only one way to do it.

The tower stood as she had seen it that first morning when she had come looking for him, the butter-coloured stone a little more dusty, the flush of spring flowers already past their best. It was time for the hardier geraniums and oleanders to soften its stark lines.

As she stood before the great front door her head-long rush back to the island to warn Chay seemed foolhardy in the extreme. He might shut the door in her face, refuse to speak to her. But she had to try.

She raised her hand to the antique dolphin knocker, but before she could announce her presence the door was flung open and Theresa, white-faced, gave a little scream.

'Miss Sophie! *Dio grazzi!*' Then she looked around. 'Where is Mr Chay?'

'Isn't he here?'

Theresa's eyes rolled. 'No, he is——' She stopped. 'You must come. Help me,' she said breathlessly. Then retreated into her own language.

'Theresa!' The sharp tone in Sophie's voice shocked the woman into silence. 'Tell me! What is the matter?' The woman pointed to the cliff, then buried her face in her apron. Sophie followed the gesture, a slight frown creasing her forehead. Then, with a sudden unease that fastened itself around her heart and wouldn't let go, she grabbed Theresa's arm. 'Is it Chay? Is he on the cliff?' Theresa began to wail pitifully, shaking her head, and suddenly Sophie knew. 'Oh, no. Please, God, no.' The words were wrenched from her. 'Where is Chay?'

'Gone. . . He's gone. . .' Her eyes were rolling, and it was obvious the woman was beyond sense. Kicking off her high-heeled shoes, Sophie began to run. Down the path to the beach, along by the cave and then over the rocks, taking care not to slip. The thought that Tom needed her help, that there was no one else, made her slow when all she wanted to do was race.

She caught her breath as she saw him. About thirty feet up and very still, his face chalk-white. He looked so small.

'Tom' she called, very gently, very evenly. 'I'm coming up to you. Just hold on.'

He didn't move, didn't speak. He was clearly too frightened even to move his head. She looked for a way to get to him and then, with a swift prayer to whatever saint looked after fools and little children, she grasped the handhold that offered itself so invitingly. But she was not a dare-devil boy. Nothing would have tempted her on to the cliff-face again. Only love.

It was a slow and painful climb for unaccustomed limbs, but she had learned her lesson the last time. If she tried to rush she would never make it. And, for Tom's sake, she had to make it. Foot by foot she moved towards him. It wasn't a difficult climb if you didn't look down or think about the drop. Or Matt Buchanan falling to his death as his brother tried to reach him.

Tom began to wail just before she reached him. A long thin sound that cut her to the heart and lent a desperate speed to her hands and feet. Then she was beside him. 'Hi, pardner,' she said softly. His face began to crack, but she didn't want him to cry. He would have to participate in his own rescue or they were both in trouble, and she quickly moved her body over Tom's, so that he would feel her at his back, protecting him, and almost at once he seemed to relax a little. 'Shall we see if we can get on to the ledge?' she suggested, and after a long moment he nodded, once.

Her first thought had been to take him back down. At least the drop reduced with every step. But, having climbed so far, she was certain that neither of them would make it, and the ledge was only a few feet further on. For a moment she glanced up, half hoping to see Chay's familiar face, the strong hand extended to help. Then she gritted her teeth. No one was going to help them.

She felt for a handhold and found a likely lump of rock. It held firm and she pulled herself up, and showed Tom where to put his hands. It worked, and, confidence restored a little, he allowed her to help him until he was perched on the ledge and he, at least, was safe.

For a moment she remained where she was, aching, sore and deeply frightened, but she knew she would have to make the effort to join the boy on the ledge before her own strength gave out. She reached for a rocky protrusion, an ideal handhold from which to pull herself up, but as she shifted her weight it gave way. Clawing momentarily at space, her heartbeat rattling in panic, sweat standing out in beads on her forehead and upper lip, she knew she was going to die.

Then her clutching fingers found something solid and stuck fast. Tom lunged to help her. 'Get back,' she yelled sharply. As she saw the pinched white face leaning above her, she swallowed and tried to smile. 'Sorry, Tom. I'll be fine. Just sit right back, away from the ledge. I'll just have a little rest.' She tried to ignore the sweat gathering under her fingers and the pain in her chest. The sense of *déjà vu* was almost overhwelming. 'Chay,' she whispered fervently, but this time Chay wasn't there to rescue her.

'Can I offer you a hand, Sophie Nash?' She jerked out of a half-faint. She was beginning to imagine things as her need for him conjured the words from her brain. Yet the gentle voice had sounded so real that she was unable to stop herself glancing up to the cliff-top, but there was no one there. She glanced at Tom, cowering back on the ledge. At least he was safe, she thought. She had done that for Chay. That was all that mattered, and she laid her forehead against the rock.

Then Chay was there beside her, his arm was around her, and she was being propelled upwards on to the ledge beside the boy.

'Chay?' She stared into the grim white mask of his face. 'Where did you come from? Theresa said——'

He indicated the top of the cliff a few yards above them. 'Shall we adjourn the inquest until you're both safe?' he interrupted abruptly. 'Sit there and don't move. I'll come back for you.'

Then he made Tom stand and slowly, carefully, coaxed him to climb the rest of the way. To Sophie it was agony, watching as the two of them covered the distance, Chay's calm voice indicating the best route and Tom, confidence recovering fast, putting his hands and feet where he was told, unaware of the hand at his back ready to grasp him. Why on earth didn't he just carry him up? Dump him over the edge and make sure he was safe?

Finally it was done, and she let out a long, slow shuddering breath and felt all the tension slide out of her body.

'Now it's your turn, Sophie Nash.' And there was no doubt from his expression that it had been a mistake to return. He was still angry with her. Very angry.

'I can manage,' she said stubbornly, as he ordered her to put her arms about his neck.

'Can you?' he said sharply. 'I don't think so.' Then, his voice a little gentler, 'Perhaps you should let me help.' And her heart began to beat a little faster.

'Despite the undoubted provocation?'

'Despite everything. Come on, Sophie, let's go home.' And together they climbed to the top. He made no effort to disguise his help. Her ego was long beyond the need of such protection. His hand was there behind her all the way. Steadying, comforting, reassuring. Then he was hauling her over the ledge.

Tom was waiting. Theresa too, crouched over the boy, crying, wiping her eyes with her apron, her arms cradling him, rocking him. But when Tom saw Sophie he broke away.

'You've come back, Sophie,' he said, flinging himself at her, all terror apparently forgotten. 'Will you stay now? You won't go away again?'

'Tom!' Chay's voice was sharp. 'Haven't you got something to say to Sophie?'

Tom's face fell. 'I. . . I'm sorry, Sophie.'

'Are you?' She gathered him in and hugged him. 'I do understand,' she whispered. 'It was a challenge. Something you had to do.' His dark eyes looked at her uncertainly, and then she knew why Chay had made the boy climb the last few yards himself. 'But now it's done,' she said. 'You've climbed the cliff like Uncle Matt and Papa and you'll never have to do it again.' She saw the flicker of relief touch the child's eyes before he threw his arms about her neck, and she felt the little body tremble against her.

Then Chay picked him up and held him close for a moment, before handing him over to Theresa. 'Take him back to the cottage, Theresa, and stick him in the bath,' he recommended. 'Then give him something to eat. He must be hungry.' He ruffled the boy's hair. 'Go on, Tom. We'll come down and see you later.'

'Why is he going to the cottage?'

'All his things are there. I arranged for him to stay down with Theresa and Twany while I was in London.'

She stared at him. 'But you're not in London.'

'No,' he said. 'I'm not.'

'Chay——' she began. 'I know you're still angry——'

'Angry? Of course I'm angry.' She stepped back as if slapped, and he swore. 'Oh, Sophie,' he said fiercely, catching her and pulling her close against his chest to bury his face in her hair. 'I'm not angry with you. You risked your life to save Tom. It wasn't as if you didn't know. . .' He gave a long, painful shudder. 'I'm angry with myself for not realising how serious he was. You did warn me.' He straightened, held her at arm's length and finally managed a lop-sided smile. 'We really must stop meeting like this.'

'Twice is more than enough,' she agreed, her heart-rate racketing dangerously out of control.

'At least I don't have to carry you this time.' He put his arm around her shoulder. 'Or do I?' He frowned. 'You're trembling.'

'I'm s-s-sorry.' And then her teeth were rattling and she was shivering and her legs were like rubber. He swore and swung her up into his arms. 'Come on. I think we could both do with a large brandy.'

She peeped up at him from under a curtain of long thick lashes and took the biggest risk of her life. Far worse than climbing the cliff, the consequences of misjudgement just as final. 'You promised me champagne. . .once.'

He stood her, very carefully, on the living-room floor, and turned her into his arms. 'So I did. You shall have bottles of the stuff. You can bath in it if you want to, but not right now. Right now there's someone you have to meet.'

He turned her round, and for a moment she didn't understand. A young fair-haired woman stepped towards her, oddly familiar and yet. . . 'Hello, Sophie.'

'Jennie?' Sophie took an uncertain step forward. Then she flew to her, hugging her, crying and laughing all at once. 'Oh, Jennie.' Then she saw the smaller, younger Jennie, hiding shyly behind her mother.

'This is Kate.'

Sophie bent down. 'Hello, Kate. I'm your Aunt Sophie.'

The child touched her face. 'You're just like my mummy.'

'Yes, darling. Exactly like.'

'Come on, Kate. Mummy and Sophie have a lot to talk about.' Chay took the child's hand. 'We'll go and find Tom and he can show you his pony. He might even let you sit on her.'

It was a long time later, hours in reality, years in words, before they finally stopped talking and went to look for Chay and Kate and Tom. The three of them were in the cottage having supper, and Theresa waved them into seats and produced two more plates.

'Chay. . .'

'Later, Sophie. We'll talk later.' When we're on our own, his eyes promised, and her face grew warm.

'But I don't understand. Why did you bring Jennie here?'

'Because when I took her to your flat, your next-door neighbour told me you had rushed off to Malta on some emergency. This was the contact address she had. So we followed you.' He frowned. 'Why. . .?'

But Sophie had already leapt to her feet. 'Oh, lord,

I forgot. . .in all the excitement. Nigel stole a photograph of you and Tom from my flat. . .'

'When?'

'This morning. . .'

He didn't waste time asking what photograph or
when she had taken it. 'Excuse us, Jennie.' He rose
and took her arm. 'Tell me,' he demanded as he strode
with her back up to the tower, and a little breathlessly
she explained what had happened.

There was a newly installed telephone on the desk in
his study and he punched in a number.

'Poppy? Chay Buchanan. Don't talk, just listen. I
want you to call the editor of *Celebrity*. He's going to
be offered a photograph of me with Tom by someone
called Nigel Phillips. It's stolen. Tell him if they use it
he'll be charged as an accessory.' He listened for a
moment. 'Well, just in case he's prepared to take the
risk, you'd better issue a press release. You can
announce a new Chay Buchanan novel for the autumn
list. The first part of a trilogy——' He broke off as there
was a burst of excitement from the receiver. 'Yes, yes.
You'll have the manuscript by courier. And you can
also mention that I'm getting married.' He glanced at
Sophie as she made a choked sound. 'You've met the
bride.' He grinned at her. 'Yes, it's Mary Poppins.
When? Well, I've got the licence in my pocket, so
don't bother to ring back, because we'll be on our
honeymoon.' He took Sophie's hand and pulled her
closer. 'Where?' He laughed softly. 'My dear Poppy,
that information is classified.' He pressed the cut-off
button and put the receiver on his desk.

'Chay. . .' Sophie protested, a little breathlessly.
'You can't. . . You mustn't. All that publicity. . . It'll
destroy everything you've worked for. . .'

'No, my love. Did you doubt for a moment that once

his grandfather had met Tom he could fail to love him?'

'It went well?'

'The first few minutes were a bit sticky. Then. . . Well, you know Tom.' He captured her chin and tilted it until she was completely at his mercy. 'And you know me. I warned you once that I was prepared to keep you here for as long as I had to.'

'Imprisoned at the top of your tower?' she asked, a little shakily.

'If necessary. I'm going to ask you a question. I'd like the answer to be yes.'

'But I have to explain.'

'No, you don't. You said that you would never do anything to hurt Tom or me. "Believe me," you said. I should never have doubted you. Can you forgive me?'

'There's nothing to——'

'I want to hear you say yes. Can you forgive me?'

'Yes, Chay,' she said.

'Convince me,' he insisted, pulling her into his arms.

Slowly, a little shyly, she raised her hands to cradle his face and stood on tiptoe to kiss him. It was so sweet, so wonderful, like rain after a drought. 'Is that convincing enough?' she asked at last, a little breathlessly.

'We'll come back to that one.' He took her hands. 'I'll tell you at length, when I've less important things on my mind, just how I found Jennie. But with friends who have access to the right computers——'

'How on earth did you know that was what it was all about?'

'Something he said. *Remember Jennie*. I checked up on Phillips. He's done this sort of thing before. A very nasty piece of work.'

'He said he had found her in one of those awful bed and breakfast places. . .'

'He lied.'

'Yes. I was very stupid to have ever believed him.'

'No, darling. You were vulnerable. People who care are always at the mercy of the unscrupulous. But we shouldn't be too hard on him.'

'Why not?' she demanded indignantly.

'Because without him we would have never met. And I would never have been able to ask you to marry me. Will you marry me?'

'This is where you want me to say yes?' she asked, her voice breaking a little.

'You're catching on, my darling.'

'Am I?' She slid her arms around his neck and a little smile played about her mouth. 'Convince me, Chay.'

And it was some time later before she was able to gaze up into that fierce, proud, wonderful face. For a moment the whole world held its breath and waited. 'Yes, Chay,' she said. 'Yes, please.'

New from Harlequin Romance
a very special six-book series by

The town of Hard Luck, Alaska, needs women!

The O'Halloran brothers, who run a bush-plane service called **Midnight Sons**, are heading a campaign to attract women to Hard Luck. *(Location: north of the Arctic Circle. Population: 150—mostly men!)*

"Debbie Macomber's *Midnight Sons* series is a delightful romantic saga. And each book is a powerful, engaging story in its own right. Unforgettable!"

—Linda Lael Miller

TITLE IN THE MIDNIGHT SONS SERIES:

Harlequin Romance ®

brings you

HOLDING
HER⭐
OUT FOR A

Some men are worth waiting for!

They're handsome, they're charming but, best of all,
they're single! Twelve lucky women are about to
discover that finding Mr. Right is not a problem—it's
holding on to him.

In May the series continues with:

#3408 MOVING IN WITH ADAM
by Jeanne Allan

Hold out for Harlequin Romance's heroes in
coming months...

◊ June: **THE DADDY TRAP**—Leigh Michaels

◆ July: **THE BACHELOR'S WEDDING**—Betty Neels

◆ August: **KIT AND THE COWBOY**—Rebecca Winters

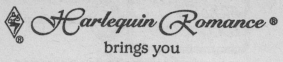
Harlequin Romance ®

brings you

How the West Was Wooed!

We've rounded up twelve of our most popular authors, and the result is a whole year of romance, Western style. Every month we'll be bringing you a spirited, independent woman whose heart is about to be lassoed by a rugged, handsome, one-hundred-percent cowboy!

Watch for...

- ♦ May: THE BADLANDS BRIDE—Rebecca Winters
- ♦ June: RUNAWAY WEDDING—Ruth Jean Dale
- ♦ July: A RANCH, A RING AND EVERYTHING—Val Daniels
- ♦ August: TEMPORARY TEXAN—Heather Allison

Available wherever Harlequin books are sold.

BRIDE'S BAY RESORT

UNLOCK THE DOOR TO GREAT ROMANCE AT BRIDE'S BAY RESORT

Join Harlequin's new across-the-lines series, set in an exclusive hotel on an island off the coast of South Carolina.

Seven of your favorite authors will bring you exciting stories about fascinating heroes and heroines discovering love at Bride's Bay Resort.

Look for these fabulous stories coming to a store near you beginning in January 1996.

Harlequin American Romance #613 in January
Matchmaking Baby by Cathy Gillen Thacker

Harlequin Presents #1794 in February
Indiscretions by Robyn Donald

Harlequin Intrigue #362 in March
Love and Lies by Dawn Stewardson

Harlequin Romance #3404 in April
Make Believe Engagement by Day Leclaire

Harlequin Temptation #588 in May
Stranger in the Night by Roseanne Williams

Harlequin Superromance #695 in June
Married to a Stranger by Connie Bennett

Harlequin Historicals #324 in July
Dulcie's Gift by Ruth Langan

Visit Bride's Bay Resort each month wherever Harlequin books are sold.

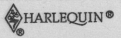

HARLEQUIN®

BBAYG